So…no.

Sophie was not for him.

Who cared if those plump lips of hers just begged to be kissed? Who cared that her curves still had the power to cause him to squirm? Who cared if he couldn't seem to banish her from his mind…or his dreams?

Because he *was* dreaming of her. The other night he'd relived the first time they'd met and the first time they'd made love. It had been so real, he'd been unable to shake the feeling that his subconscious was trying to tell him something.

No.

He couldn't go there.

He had to forget about her.

There were plenty of other sexy, beautiful and intelligent women out there. He did not have to get entangled with someone who would cause him only grief. He could do this. He could forget about Sophie. It was mind over matter, just as everything was.

Decision made.

Dillon would shove sexy Sophie out of his mind.

Permanently.

Oh, Baby!

PATRICIA KAY

First published in Great Britain 2015
by Mills & Boon, an imprint of Harlequin (UK) Limited,
Large Print edition 2015
Eton House, 18-24 Paradise Road,
Richmond, Surrey, TW9 1SR

ISBN: 978-0-263-25994-0

Harlequin (UK) Limited's policy is to use papers that are natural, renewable and recyclable products and made from wood grown in sustainable forests. The logging and manufacturing processes conform to the legal environmental regulations of the country of origin.

Printed and bound in Great Britain
by CPI Antony Rowe, Chippenham, Wiltshire

PATRICIA KAY

Formerly writing as Trisha Alexander, Patricia Kay is a *USA TODAY* bestselling author of more than forty-eight novels of contemporary romance and women's fiction. She lives in Houston, Texas. To learn more about her, visit her website at patriciakay.com.

This book is dedicated, with much love,
to my three sisters: Gerri Paulicivic,
Marge Ford and Norma Johnson.
And to my sisters-in-law, who are
equally wonderful: Susan Kay Ardale,
Beverly Kay, A. Kay Kay and Theresa Kay.
I am so lucky to have all of you in my life.

Chapter One

Crandall Lake, Texas—early October

Sophie Marlowe sneaked a glance at the clock. Eleven thirty-five. Twenty-five minutes until her lunch break. Suppressing a sigh, she turned her attention back to the student sitting in front of her desk. “What are you going to do, Kaitlyn?”

The unhappy senior shrugged. “I don’t know.”

“They’re going to have to be told sometime.

It would be best if you just tell them now while you still have options."

The girl nodded, her eyes bleak. "They're gonna kill me."

Sophie smiled wryly. "I know your parents. They are lovely, rational people. They won't kill you."

"But they'll be so disappointed," Kaitlyn muttered.

"I'm sure they will, but they love you. They'll get over it." Yet even as Sophie said the rote words, she knew that some parents didn't *get over it* easily. When your daughter was smart, got great grades and was on track to attend one of the best universities in Texas, it was hard to discover said daughter wasn't as smart as you'd thought. That, in fact, she was pregnant and already a couple of months along.

"I wish…" Kaitlyn began.

"I know. You wish this hadn't happened."

Two fat tears rolled down Kaitlyn's cheeks. "Billy's being so mean to me."

Now Sophie *did* sigh. She wasn't surprised that the father of the baby wasn't thrilled by his girlfriend's pregnancy. Honestly. What in the world were these kids *thinking*? That was the problem. They weren't thinking. The thinking began after the damage was done, and by then, it was too late. "Would you like me to be with you when you talk to your parents?" As Crandall Lake High School's guidance counselor, Sophie wasn't required to do more than listen to and advise students of available resources, but she couldn't help feeling sorry for the girl in her office. Kaitlyn Lowe was a good kid. In fact, she was one of the last kids Sophie thought would be in this position.

"Would you?"

The raw fear in Kaitlyn's blue eyes reminded Sophie that the girl was only seventeen. *Only a year older than Joy.* The thought of Joy, her younger half sister and legal ward, whose parents had died two years earlier, gave Sophie further pause. If it were Joy sitting here now, scared and feeling so alone, wouldn't Sophie want someone to befriend her, too? "Yes," she said softly. "I will."

"Oh, Miss Marlowe, thank you. Wh-when do you want to do it?"

Sophie had book club tonight, but tomorrow was free. "Why don't I come by tomorrow night? Say about seven-thirty? Will you be through with dinner by then?"

Kaitlyn nodded, then bit her bottom lip.

Later, as Sophie ate her tuna sandwich and apple in the teachers' lounge, she thought about how hard it was to be a teenager. She was certainly glad those days were long behind her. And she was enormously grateful that Joy had lived up to her name and was a joy to raise. The girl had never given Sophie one moment of trouble, thank the Lord.

She looked up at the noisy entrance of two of her colleagues—Ann McPherson, a chemistry teacher, and Cindy Bloom, who taught computer science and keyboarding.

"Oh God," Cindy said, fanning herself, "be still, my heart!"

"Yeah," Ann said. "He's gorgeous, isn't he? And I'm sure he knows it."

"Of course he knows it!" Cindy said, laughing. "I mean, he's dated some of the most beautiful women in the world."

Sophie kept her expression blank, even though she instantly knew the two women were discussing Dillon Burke, former pro quarterback for the Los Angeles Lions, who had moved back to his hometown of Crandall

Lake in June and was now the new varsity football coach at the high school. The very same Dillon Burke with whom she, Sophie, had once been wildly in love.

And who she was now avoiding at all costs.

Our relationship took place a long time ago, she reminded herself for about the hundredth time since she'd heard he'd come back to town. *He's no longer even a blip on your radar screen.* And if she'd had any doubts that this was so, the fact that he hadn't made any effort at all to see her or talk to her would have made that fact abundantly clear.

Unfortunately, the nonblip had gotten nonstop publicity and attention ever since he hit town. Sophie would have had to be blind not to notice he was even better-looking now than he'd been as a senior in high school. Tall, with black hair and piercing blue eyes and a body to die for, he had set many a heart aflutter in the past thirteen years.

But not mine! I'm so over him.

Sophie was just grateful that most of her colleagues had never known she and Dillon were once an item. And the few who had known must feel the way Sophie felt now: that the relationship between her as a sixteen-year-old sophomore and Dillon, as a senior and the star quarterback of Crandall High's Cougars, was nothing more than a teenage fling long forgotten by everyone.

"It won't be any different here," Ann was saying. "I noticed Nicole was all over him at the fair Saturday."

Cindy grimaced. "She makes me sick."

They were discussing Nicole Blanchard, the French teacher. New this year, she'd been a topic of speculation from the first day of school—leggy, blond and gorgeous. Every man who came into her orbit fell under her spell. Sophie figured Dillon Burke would be no different.

"Yeah, well, he didn't seem to be unhappy about the attention." Finally noticing Sophie, Ann said, "Hey, Sophie, how's it going?"

"Okay. How about you?" Finishing her sandwich, Sophie started on her apple.

"Well, I'm tired from the weekend. Other than that, things are great."

They continued with meaningless chitchat for a few more minutes, and then Sophie said, "I think I'll take a walk. See you guys later." She pitched her apple core into the trash, stood and dusted off her jeans, then waved goodbye.

Outside, even though it was already the first week of October and should be cooling off by now, the temperature today was supposed to reach eighty-five. Sophie had lived in Texas her entire life, but she'd never become used to the heat. Maybe it was her redheaded complexion, but the only time of the year she truly enjoyed living in the area was in the winter. She'd often thought she'd be happier in a northern state somewhere and had even toyed with applying to schools in Michigan, Ohio or Pennsylvania. She'd fantasized about settling in a bigger city, somewhere she might have a better chance of meeting the kind of guy she still hoped to one day find.

But then her mother and Joy's dad, Josh—Sophie's stepdad—were killed in the plane crash, and Sophie became Joy's legal guardian. All thoughts of moving away had been shelved. Keeping Joy's life as close to normal as possible became Sophie's number-one priority…and always would be until Joy was out of college and able to take care of herself.

Sophie was so caught up in her thoughts that as she rounded the corner on her way to the side entrance of the school, which was closest to her office, she collided with someone coming the other way.

"Oh, sorry," she said, looking up.

"Sorry," he said, looking down.

Hazel's eyes locked with blue eyes, and for one long moment, Sophie didn't breathe.

"Well, well, well," Dillon Burke said, a smile playing around his mouth. "If it isn't Sophie Marlowe. I was beginning to think you were a figment of my imagination."

Sophie's traitorous heart skipped alarmingly as she tried to think of something clever to say. "Hello, Dillon" was all she could manage.

He grinned. "Hello, Sophie."

"I, um, was on my way back to my office." Oh, great. Was that the best she could do?

"So I see."

He was still smiling, and his eyes—oh, those eyes!—were giving her a thorough once-over.

"I, uh, heard you were back." Dear Lord. Now she sounded like an idiot. *I heard you were back*. No, duh.

He made a face. "You and everyone else in Texas."

"That's what happens when you're famous."

"Famous." He made the word sound like a curse.

"You hadn't seemed to mind the attention in the past."

"*Past* being the operative word."

Sophie pointedly looked at her watch. "Well, it's nice seeing you again, Dillon. But I need to get back to work."

Giving her a little bow to go along with his sexy smile, he said, drawling a little to sho his Texas roots, "Good to see you, too, Sophie. And by the way, you're lookin' good." His gaze moved to her butt. "I can remember when jeans that fit like yours were outlawed."

Sophie could feel the blush heating her face. She could also feel his eyes watching her as she made her escape through the side door.

Thank God no one had seen their encounter. Because Sophie was sure if anyone had, they'd have immediately known she was not immune to the charms of Dillon Burke, no matter how many times she told herself she was.

Man, she was one sexy woman. Dillon couldn't get over how good Sophie looked. Nor could he get over how much seeing her had affected him. This wasn't the first time he'd had a glimpse of her, but it was their first close encounter. The first time he'd been able to see those beautiful gold-flecked eyes, that smattering of freckles across her nose and cheeks, the way her full lower lip looked ready and ripe....

Damn. Best not to go there.

She'd been avoiding him. Truth to tell, he'd been avoiding her, too. Not that he had anything to regret where she was concerned. He'd been up front with her from the beginning. He'd made her no promises. She'd always known he was going off to college when he graduated.

And he did. Pretty much without a backward glance. Oh, he'd thought about Sophie. He couldn't help thinking about her. They'd been a pretty steady item for nearly a year, and he'd fallen hard for her. It had taken him months, years actually, to stop comparing other women to her. And if he was being completely honest, he'd never really stopped. No matter who he was with, somehow he always had Sophie in the back of his mind as his gold standard.

Had anyone else ever measured up?

Tessa, maybe, for a while at least. Until she got greedy.

And Leeann until she let slip one day that she had no interest in kids. Never wanted any. Had made sure she'd never have any. That had been the end of Leeann. That had been the end of models, period.

Nowadays, he wasn't sure he wanted any kind of involvement with women. Just handling all the problems that went along with raising an eighteen-year-old boy was enough to keep him hopping. Dillon sighed, thinking of his nephew, Aidan. Aidan's father, a career marine who had been Dillon's oldest brother, had been killed in Afghanistan five years ago, and his mother had died of colon cancer in January. Since then, Aidan had been Dillon's responsibility.

Under normal circumstances, everything might have worked out fine, because Aidan—

recent evidence to the contrary—was a good kid. But the trauma of losing his last parent and having to move from everything familiar to a town thousands of miles from the only home he'd ever known right before his senior year, *and* having to get used to an uncle he had barely seen in the past ten years, had proved to be Aidan's undoing.

In fact, Dillon wasn't sure the two of them were going to make it. No matter what rules Dillon laid down, Aidan simply ignored them. If he was told to be in no later than midnight on the weekends, he would show up at one… or later.

Punishment seemed to have no effect. Dillon had tried withholding spending money, taking away the car keys, grounding Aidan completely—nothing worked. Aidan seemed determined to push the boundaries to the limit, and nothing Dillon did or said made any difference to him.

Intellectually, Dillon knew that Aidan was acting out because it was the only way he could feel in control of at least some part of his life. But knowing what was causing the bad behavior didn't make it any easier to deal with.

If only Dillon had someone to talk to. He'd actually considered confiding in Sophie. After all, she was the guidance counselor at Crandall Lake High School. Who better to talk to? But every time he had considered approaching her, he got cold feet. Getting cold feet over talking to a woman was a new experience for Dillon. And it wasn't a feeling he liked.

By now Dillon had reached his own office, down the hall from the gym and across from the boys' locker room. Inside he saw his assistant coach, Brian Penner, waiting. Time to stop thinking about Aidan and start thinking about Friday night's game.

"Hey, Dillon, we need to talk," Brian said, his affable face sporting a worried frown.

"What's up?" Dillon said, dropping the load of files he'd carried from the main office onto his already-littered desk.

"It's Jimmy."

Crap. Jimmy Ferguson was the Cougars' quarterback. Right now he was sidelined with a knee injury, and even though the knee was healing nicely and Jimmy should be able to play again by the end of the month, the kid wasn't handling his inactivity well. He'd caused one problem after another in the past few weeks, and Dillon was seriously considering banishing him from the locker room as well as the field.

"You know what the problem is," Brian said.

"Yeah." If the team hadn't been doing well during Ferguson's forced absence, things would probably be fine—at least as far as Jimmy was concerned. However, the team *was* doing well. In fact, they'd won their last two games, mostly because their backup quarterback, Devon Washington, had performed spectacularly. Dillon knew Jimmy was worried he'd lose his starting spot if things continued to go well while he was sidelined.

"We need to do something," Brian said, plopping down on a corner of Dillon's desk.

Dillon sank into his leather armchair and sighed. "I know. I just hate to make an example of him. It's hard enough for the kid right now."

"Yeah, but if the other guys see him getting away with this crap, that's not good, either."

"I know." Jeez, Dillon was beginning to wonder if he was cut out for this coaching gig. Or for the fatherhood gig he'd found himself in. And yet what choice did he have? It was important to establish a stable home for Aidan and it was just as important to establish some kind of stable career for himself. He was damned if he wanted to become one of those ex-jocks who tried to become actors or spent their days pitching products nobody needed. And he had no interest in spending his days in a monkey suit and tie, either. He sighed again. "I'll talk to him, Brian. I'll make it clear he's on notice, and if he keeps causing trouble, he'll be kicked off the team for good."

Brian nodded. His still-worried expression mirrored Dillon's own misgivings. Because Dillon knew removing Jimmy Ferguson—the cosseted and spoiled only son of Crandall Lake's mayor—from the varsity football squad in his senior year would cause a huge uproar in the community. And Dillon had enough strife in his life right now.

Joy Ferrelli yawned, then glanced longingly out the window. If only she'd been able to skip school today the way Aidan had wanted her to. Any one of her friends could've gotten away with it, but they didn't have older sisters teaching here as she did. No way Joy could skip school without Sophie finding out about it.

Sophie would have a cow if she knew about Joy and Aidan. That was the biggest reason for keeping their relationship a secret, but it wasn't the only one. Truth was, Joy didn't want to share what she had with Aidan. She didn't want her girlfriends teasing her about him or asking her questions or giving her advice.

She especially didn't want them *guessing*,

although she was afraid they probably had guessed. Megan, her BFF, had hinted as much the other day, but Joy had managed to squirm out of a direct answer. That probably wouldn't be the case much longer, especially because it was getting harder and harder to disguise the way Joy felt about Aidan.

She thought about last night. The way she'd sneaked out of her room after Sophie went to bed. The way Aidan was waiting for her at the corner of the street. The way they could barely wait to get to the lake before making love. And it *was* making love. Joy refused to even think of their relationship and the sex between them any other way. What they did was romantic and wonderful…and, and…*beautiful.* She guessed that was why she didn't want anyone else to know. Because even Megan might snicker and give her sly looks and say something that would belittle what she had with Aidan. No, Joy couldn't bear that.

Joy sighed, remembering how Aidan always made her feel. And how much she loved him.

"Miss Ferrelli, would it be too much to ask you to answer my question?"

Joy blinked. "Huh?"

"That's what I thought," Mr. Gardner said, frowning. "You didn't even *hear* the question." He shook his head, obviously disgusted. "If this class is that boring, maybe you'd like to drop it and take something more to your liking."

Joy swallowed. American history was a required subject for sophomores. She couldn't drop it, and old sour-face Gardner knew it. "Sorry, Mr. Gardner. I—I didn't sleep well last night. I promise it won't happen again."

"Hmmph. See that it doesn't." He gave her

his fish-eyed stare. "Or you'll find yourself in detention."

For a while, Joy forced herself to pay attention, even though she'd much rather have relived the night before. Where was Aiden now? she wondered. Had he skipped out? Had he gone out to the lake? Was he sitting in the sun, smoking a little weed?

That was another thing that would cause Sophie to have a fit, Joy thought, squirming inside. If her sister'd had any clue Joy was smoking pot once in a while, she'd…Joy didn't know *what* she'd do. Probably ground Joy for the rest of her life. Plus, she'd be so disappointed. Joy could imagine the look Sophie would get on her face. And even though Joy was totally in love with Aiden and didn't really see anything wrong with having some weed now and then—after all, what was the big deal, anyway?—she loved Sophie, and she didn't want her to get upset.

So quit, then. Tell Aiden the truth. That you don't like him smoking weed and you're not going to do it with him anymore.

"Miss Ferrelli! I told you earlier if you were bored, you could leave this class. I'm sending a note to the office. Report to Mrs. Woodsen immediately."

Joy's heart lodged somewhere in her throat. She couldn't believe she'd drifted into another daydream. Face flaming—how she hated the way she blushed so easily—she hastily gathered her books and mumbled, "Sorry, Mr. Gardner. Sorry."

"That's what you said the last time." He didn't look up from his cell phone where he was texting the office.

Joy swallowed. *Oh God.* Now she was in for it. On top of the detention she'd almost certainly get, Sophie was bound to punish her. And Friday night was homecoming. Joy had been planning to actually tell Sophie she had been invited to go by Aiden, kind of test the waters. Now she'd be lucky if Sophie let her go anywhere this weekend, let alone on a date with a senior boy.

You've totally screwed up.

Joy just hoped her sister was in a good mood tonight. Maybe the fact that Joy had never caused Sophie any problems before would make a difference. Maybe Sophie would be in a forgiving mood and Joy would get away with no more than a talking-to.

Sighing heavily, Joy headed for the office and whatever fate awaited her.

Chapter Two

"You *what*?" Sophie said, staring at Joy.

Joy grimaced. "I got sent to the office because I wasn't paying attention in history class."

"I don't believe it. You of all people. Why, I thought you loved history."

"I do love history. What I don't love is old sourpuss Gardner."

"Don't call him that. It's disrespectful." Sophie kept her expression neutral, even though privately she had called Philip Gardner worse. He was more than a sourpuss. He was downright nasty.

"I'm sorry. But he's so *mean.*"

"No excuses, Joy. You weren't paying attention in class, and Mr. Gardner was perfectly justified in sending you to the office. So, what happened there?"

"Mrs. Woodson gave me a week's detention."

"Good." Connie Woodson was the assistant principal.

Joy hung her head. "I'm sorry, Sophie. I really am. It won't happen again."

Sophie suppressed a smile. She knew why Joy was so apologetic. She didn't want to be punished by Sophie, too. "You're not going to escape punishment because you've apologized, you know."

Joy bit her bottom lip. Her eyes, the same

soft blue as their mother's, never failed to elicit tenderness and sympathy in Sophie, although she fought to conceal it.

"I should ground you," Sophie said.

"Please don't. Not now."

Sophie knew exactly why Joy had said *not now.* Homecoming was Saturday night. And Joy wanted to go. Of course she did. All her friends would be going. Weakening, Sophie said, "Well...if you promise..."

"I do! I promise! I'll pay so much attention in *all* my classes, I'll bring home straight A's this semester."

Sophie chuckled. "Don't make promises you can't keep, sweetie."

Joy gave her a sheepish grin. "I'll make you proud, Sophie."

Sophie sighed. "Oh, all right. I won't ground you...*this time.* But see this doesn't happen again."

"It won't."

"So you have a date for homecoming? Is that why you're so eager to go?" Sophie picked up the mail, which Joy had placed on the gate-legged table in the entryway of the home that had belonged to Joy's parents.

"Um, sort of…"

Sophie idly leafed through the advertisements and credit card offers. When would these banks quit sending her this stuff? She never responded. Suddenly realizing that Joy was standing there quietly, Sophie looked up. "Sorry. I wasn't paying attention. What did you say?"

"Um, I said I did kind of have a date."

"Oh? Who with?"

"Um, Aidan Burke?"

Sophie blinked. Aidan Burke? Dillon Burke's nephew? Alarm bells began ringing in her brain. She opened her mouth, then closed it, not sure what to say. Her first instinct had been to say *over my dead body,* but she knew she would have to justify an answer like that, and what could she say? *I don't want you seeing anyone even remotely connected to Dillon Burke. The Burke men are bad news. Really bad news.* Sighing again, she met Joy's hopeful gaze. "How old is this Aidan Burke?"

Joy's expression became hesitant. "He's a senior," she said softly.

"Yes, that's what I thought." *Oh God. Is history repeating itself?* "I don't think it's a good idea for you to date a senior, Joy."

"Why? He's really nice, Sophie. You'd like him."

Sophie could just imagine. She'd seen Dillon's nephew from a distance. He was a good-looking kid. In fact, he reminded her of Dillon when *he* was a kid. No. This would never do. "You are too young to date a senior. And when did you meet him, anyway?"

"At the pool. This summer."

"I see." She studied Joy for a moment, but Joy evaded her gaze. "Have you *already* gone out with him?" At first, Sophie wasn't sure Joy was going to answer her. But then she looked up.

"We've never had a date."

There was something about Joy's answer that bothered Sophie, but she certainly wasn't going to accuse her sister of lying to her. *Was* she lying?

"Sophie, I just wish you'd meet him…"

"I'm sorry, Joy, but I've made up my mind. You cannot go to homecoming with him. You can dance with him if he asks you, but you cannot go with him or allow him to bring you home."

Joy's face crumpled. "This is so unfair. You…you don't even know him!"

"Joy," Sophie said quietly, "you knew what my reaction was going to be before you even told me about him." When Joy just stared at her, Sophie added, "We agreed last year, when you first began dating, that you would stick to boys in your age bracket."

"But that was before I'd met Aidan. Please, Sophie, just give him a chance. Let him come over and talk to you. I know you'll change your mind if you meet him."

Sophie shook her head. If Aidan had even one quarter of the charm his uncle had, she would be putty in his hands. "No, honey. It's out of the question. When you're older and in college, you can make your own choices about who you date. While you're here, and I'm in charge, the rules will stand."

Joy gave her one last beseeching look,

then walked away dejectedly. Sophie sighed. *Please, God, give me the strength to get her safely through high school.*

An hour later, dinner on the table, Sophie called upstairs to tell Joy it was time to eat. Hearing nothing in return, she called louder. When there was still no response, she climbed the stairs and knocked on Joy's bedroom door before opening it, all ready to deliver a reprimand. Her mouth instead fell open. The room was empty.

"Joy?" Sophie walked in, then checked the adjoining bathroom. Joy wasn't there. Where was she? Sophie looked at Joy's nightstand where her charger lay. Joy's cell phone, which was always connected to the charger when Joy was in the room, wasn't there, either.

Her niece had sneaked out.

Somehow Joy had come down the stairs noiselessly, opened the front door and left without making any noise or saying a word to Sophie.

Sophie's heart sped up. She was furious. In fact, she couldn't believe Joy had defied her like this. Worse, she couldn't think what she was going to do about it. Trouble was, she herself was only twenty-nine. She was too close to being a kid herself not to remember what it felt like to have a crush on an older, drop-dead-handsome boy. To think you'd die if he didn't ask you out. Maybe she'd made a terrible mistake. By telling Joy she couldn't go to homecoming with Aidan Burke, had she inadvertently pushed the girl right into his arms?

Sighing, Sophie moped downstairs. Picking up her own cell phone, she texted Joy.

Where R U? Pls come hm. Lets talk.

When ten minutes had gone by with no answer, she realized Joy either had her phone shut off or was simply going to ignore her. She probably figured Sophie wasn't going to relent on homecoming anyway, so what difference did it make? All Sophie could do was wait, and try to figure out what she was going to do now.

The house was dark when Aidan dropped Joy off. But Sophie's bedroom faced the backyard, so even if her light was still on, Joy wouldn't have been able to see it.

Joy silently let herself in, glad there was no dog to make noise, even though she'd been begging Sophie for months to let her get a Lab. Sophie had finally relented, saying they could pick out a Lab puppy for Christmas. Joy made a face. She guessed she'd probably blown *that*, too, with her disappearing act tonight.

Why had she sneaked out? She still wasn't

sure. All she knew was that when Sophie had so stubbornly refused to allow her to go to homecoming with Aidan, she was so angry she just wanted to show Sophie she couldn't control *everything* in Joy's life.

You've blown it. Totally blown it. Now she probably won't let you go to homecoming at all.

Joy was still thinking dark thoughts when she reached the top of the stairs—thankfully, not making any noise while doing it—so she wasn't fully prepared for Sophie's sudden appearance in the hallway.

"Where have you been?" Sophie demanded.

Joy swallowed. "I was upset. I—I had to get away…to think."

"To think."

"Yes." Joy straightened, abruptly deciding she would brazen this out. She was in the doghouse anyway. Might as well show some backbone.

Sophie sighed heavily. “Joy,” she began.

“I know, I know. You’re mad at me. I don’t blame you.”

“I’m more than mad, Joy. I’m disappointed. I didn’t know where you were or what you were doing. I even bailed out on my book club tonight because I was so worried about you. I’ve been sitting and waiting all night. I know you were out with that boy, otherwise I might have been tempted to call the police and have *them* look for you. The least you could have done was answer my text, let me know you were safe. I don’t think I deserve this kind of treatment from you. Do you?”

All Joy’s defiance disappeared. Instead she just felt miserable. Because her sister was right. Sophie *didn’t* deserve this kind of treatment. She was a wonderful person. A wonderful sister. And she'd never been anything but fair and kind and loving to Joy. In fact, Joy wasn't sure she would have survived losing her parents if not for Sophie. Tears stinging her eyes, Joy shook her head. "No," she whispered.

"Then why did you *do* it?"

Joy shrugged. A tear rolled down her cheek. "I—I don't know. I'm sorry, Sophie. I really am. I—deserve whatever punishment you want to give me."

Sophie nodded. She reached out and squeezed Joy's shoulder. "Look, we're both tired and upset. We won't make any decisions tonight. And we both have to be up early tomorrow. So we'll talk tomorrow night, okay?"

"Okay." Joy was grateful for the reprieve, but she was savvy enough to know that just because she'd been given some time before she had to face the music didn't mean Sophie was going to go easy on her.

Thank God it was Friday, Sophie thought as she drove to work. The week had been brutal, especially Wednesday night and last night. Thinking about last night, she hoped she'd done some good, at least for Kaitlyn, the senior who was pregnant. The meeting with Kaitlyn and her parents hadn't been easy, but at least their beautiful, college-bound daughter was in one piece. By the time Sophie had left for home, the family was in the midst of trying to make the best decision about how to go forward. The one thing all three had agreed upon was that Kaitlyn would still head off to UT next fall. Whether she would give her child up for adoption or go another direction was still up in the air.

Sophie was grateful it wasn't her decision to make. The decision she *had* made earlier, before going over to the Macpherson home, was still bothering her. She'd taken pity on Joy and hadn't forbidden her to go to homecoming, especially when Joy had meekly agreed she would attend with Megan, Jenna and Bethany, her three best friends—all of whom were going stag. Sophie had almost insisted upon picking Joy up when the evening was over, but she'd instead decided to give Joy another chance at trust.

"You're absolutely *not* to go home with Aidan Burke. You will stay with your friends and leave with your friends. Understood?"

She hoped she hadn't made a mistake, but the die was cast. And if she *had* made a mistake, and Joy disobeyed her, then that would be it. She wouldn't trust Joy again.

Driving into the teachers' parking lot,

Sophie saw a tall, dark-haired figure getting out of a black Toyota Tundra truck. Her heart skipped as she realized it was Dillon. Parking as far from his truck as it was possible, she waited until he was halfway to the entrance of the school before exiting her little Prius. She felt unsettled enough today without having to contend with another meeting with Dillon.

By the time she entered the school, he was long gone, and she headed for her office. This was one of the days she was very grateful to be the guidance counselor and entitled to a private office—minuscule as it was—rather than a teacher who could only escape into the teachers' lounge, where there was never any privacy.

The moment she entered her office, she saw the note. It was propped against her keyboard, and the handwriting on the envelope was unmistakably Principal Gordon Pearson's.

"Oh, *great*," she mumbled. "What now?"

A quick scan of the note simply told her he wanted to see her, *immediately if not sooner.* She sighed.

Dumping her tote containing the files she'd taken home, she straightened her layered tees, checked her hair to make sure it was as neat as she could make it and headed for Pearson's office.

"What's up?" she said to Janie, the principal's secretary.

"Oh, just a homecoming emergency," Janie said. "He'll tell you all about it."

Sophie frowned. Homecoming emergency? She couldn't imagine what that might be.

She didn't have to wonder long. She'd no sooner entered Principal Pearson's office than he said, "I hope you don't have plans for tomorrow night, Sophie. I need you to chaperone the homecoming dance. Jackie Farrow's mother took a turn for the worse, and she's flying to Denver this afternoon."

Jackie, a freshman math teacher, was one of the four teachers who'd drawn chaperone duty this time. And if Sophie wasn't mistaken, Dillon Burke was also a chaperone. *Oh Lord.* The last place Sophie wanted to be was a dance—with him. And from her experiences chaperoning school functions, she knew all the teachers would be seated together. There would be no way to avoid him.

For one second, she thought about fudging, saying she *did* have plans, important plans she couldn't change, but she knew that wasn't a good idea. The principal would expect her to elaborate, and she wasn't a good liar. She always stammered…or blushed…or both. She'd give herself away in an instant.

So she smothered a sigh, said, "No, I don't

have plans" and agreed that she would fill in for Jackie.

Well, she thought philosophically as she walked back to her own office, at least now she could keep tabs on Joy. Heck, she might even take advantage of having to be in Dillon's company by quizzing him about his nephew. See what she could find out about the boy.

That decided, she only had one other serious problem.

What in the world would she wear tomorrow night?

Dillon took a quick shower after the game—which Crandall Lake had won by ten points—and changed into the clothes he'd brought to wear to the homecoming dance. He wasn't thrilled about chaperoning, but when he'd tried to get out of it, Principal Pearson had been quick to let him know he had to take a turn just like everyone else on the faculty.

"It wouldn't be fair for me to let you off the hook," Pearson had said. "Would look like I think you're better than the others, and that isn't the way things work around here."

Dillon knew the man was right. He tried to operate the same way with his team. Yes, some of the players were much more talented and vital to the team, but there was no way he was going to act as if that were the case. The worst possible thing a coach could do for the morale of his team was play favorites.

Maybe it wouldn't be so bad to chaperone tonight's dance, he told himself as he headed for the ballroom where the dance would take place. It might even be fun, like reliving his own high school days.

When he arrived—later than the other chaperones since he'd had to shower and change clothes after the game—he saw the other three were already seated at their assigned table.

Oh, hell. He hadn't known Nicole Blanchard was also chaperoning tonight. The woman had been driving him crazy ever since the beginning of the school year. She followed him around, flirted shamelessly and seemed to think he welcomed it. No matter what he said or did, she didn't take the hint that he wasn't interested. She was pretty enough, but he'd only had to be in her company for one day before he knew she was bad news. If he paid her the least bit of attention, she would have them engaged and married. He'd been avoiding her as much as possible, but that would be tough to do tonight.

Then he noticed who was sitting across the table from Nicole.

Sophie.

Their eyes met and held for a brief moment;

then she abruptly stood, said something to the others and walked away. He stood there, watching her. She looked amazing. Her black dress was short and formfitting, hugging that shapely bottom of hers in a way that left nothing to the imagination. And those legs! There ought to be a law against spike heels for someone who had legs like hers.

Maybe he wasn't sorry, after all, that he was one of the four teachers working tonight.

Sophie knew it was cowardly of her, but the moment she spied Dillon walking toward their table, she'd had to get out of there, at least long enough to get her emotions—not to mention her hormones!—under some kind of control. So she'd quickly excused herself and headed for the ladies' room. While there she ran a comb through her hair—which she wore loose tonight—freshened her lipstick and given herself a fast pep talk.

You're a grown-up, not to mention a high school counselor. If you can handle hundreds of teenagers, you can certainly handle one Dillon Burke. He's not that *irresistible.*

Despite the lecture, she was still not quite prepared to face him, so she decided that while there, she might as well take care of business. She had no sooner locked herself into the end stall than several giggling girls entered the room.

"God, he's hot, isn't he?" one of them said.

"Yeah, but lot of good it does us," another commented.

"I don't know what Joy Ferrelli has that we don't," the first one said, "but Aidan hasn't even *looked* at another girl since he got to town!"

Sophie froze. She couldn't identify any of the voices.

"I know. From the moment he met her that day at the pool. She's putting out. She has to be."

"Well, if she is, Marlowe's gonna find out sooner or later, and then watch out."

Putting out? Were they *serious*? Had the relationship between Joy and Dillon's nephew gone that far? Surely it couldn't have. Why, Sophie hadn't even *known* about it until the other day. How could those kids possibly have become so involved without Sophie knowing? Crandall Lake was a small town. Sophie had thought she would immediately know if Joy was doing anything she shouldn't be doing. She'd certainly never thought allowing Joy to lifeguard at the city pool would cause problems. Why hadn't Joy mentioned meeting Aidan before now?

You know why. She knew how you'd react. If not for the fact that she wanted to come to the dance with him tonight, she probably still wouldn't have mentioned him.

It seemed to take forever for the girls to finish their business in the ladies' room and leave. When the door finally closed after them, Sophie escaped the confines of her stall, washed her hands and tried to calm herself before going out to face the others. It wasn't bad enough she had to contend with Dillon tonight. Now she had more to worry about with Joy. *Please, God. Those girls are just jealous. Don't let it be true. She's only sixteen!*

As she walked back to the teachers' table, she scanned the large ballroom, looking for her sister. It wasn't easy to spot Joy, because the DJ had put on a thumping dance anthem, and hundreds of kids were on the dance floor. But Sophie finally spied her sister, in the corner farthest from the teachers' table. And sure enough, she was with Aidan Burke. They weren't doing anything, just standing side by side, but something about the way Joy leaned into him, and the way his head tilted down so he could look into her eyes, made Sophie's heart sink.

She recognized the way they were together, because it was so similar to the way she, Sophie, had been with Dillon. Those girls were probably right. Joy and Aidan were intimate.

Oh God, Sophie thought. *I need help dealing with this.*

One thing she knew for sure. She should never have given in to Joy about tonight. She should have put her foot down and made her sister stay home. But would that have done any good? For all Sophie knew, Aidan Burke would have stayed away from the dance, too.

In fact, he could have gone over to Sophie's house and spent the entire evening there, alone with Joy, and Sophie wouldn't have been the wiser.

No, it was better to have the two of them here, where Sophie could at least see them. And as she'd planned earlier, she would find out as much as she could from Dillon about his nephew.

Then tomorrow, she would corner Joy and they would have it out. What Sophie would do from that point on, she hadn't a clue.

Chapter Three

"We thought you fell in," Nicole Blanchard said as Sophie returned to their table.

The fourth chaperone, Kevin Rafferty, who taught trig and calculus to juniors and seniors, grinned at Sophie.

Sophie smiled, determined not to let Nicole get under her skin tonight, even though the woman was hard to take, even on a good day. The trouble was, she was clueless. Her attempts at humor always fell short, and she never seemed to take a hint. Sophie noticed how now that Dillon was there and seated between Nicole and Sophie's empty seat, Nicole had scooted her chair closer to him. She wasn't even subtle.

"Did you miss me?" Sophie said mildly, taking her own seat. She noticed someone had put a drink in front of her. "What's this?" She raised the plastic glass and sniffed.

"Lemonade," Dillon said. "Other than canned drinks, that's all there is."

"Yeah," Kevin said, sighing. "Sure could use a beer."

Sophie was thinking she sure could use a margarita, but there was zero tolerance for any kind of drug, including alcohol, anywhere near a school function. Once, one of the teachers had smuggled a flask to a dance he was chaperoning and spiked his soft drink with it. Someone had seen him do it and reported him. The guy was nearly fired on the spot. Since then, there'd never been another incident.

"Thanks," Sophie said, finally looking at Dillon. Her stupid heart skittered as their eyes met once again. What was it about this man that just a glance could reduce her to jelly? Okay, so he was gorgeous and sexy. He looked especially good tonight in a white, open-necked shirt, a dark sport coat and khaki pants. And he wore some kind of woodsy cologne that Sophie loved. But still…lots of guys were hot-looking and dressed well. Normally Sophie had no problem resisting their charms. Dillon, though, was another story. Always *had* been another story. But she was determined he would never know the effect he still had on her. Nor would anyone else in her world.

Turning to Nicole, Sophie said, "I love your dress, Nicole. You look great."

"Thanks." Nicole smiled archly, all but batting her eyelashes at Dillon. Any other woman would have reciprocated the compliment, but not Nicole.

To his credit, Dillon ignored her. Instead he gave Sophie a once-over and said, "Someone else at this table looks great, too."

Sophie knew she was blushing, but thank goodness it was too dark in the ballroom for anyone else to see the telltale stain. "Thank you," she managed. "I'd say we all clean up well."

Just then, the DJ switched to a slow, romantic ballad. Not losing any time, Kevin turned toward Nicole to ask if she'd like to dance. Sophie looked at Nicole and could see by her expression that she was uncertain about whether to say yes or no, but vanity won out and she smiled, saying, "I'd love to."

Once the two of them went to the dance

floor, Dillon said, “I guess that’s our cue.” He scooted his chair back and reached for her hand.

“I don’t think—”

“You can’t say no. That would be rude.” That sexy smile of his hovered around his mouth. “Didn’t your mother teach you that?”

Sophie sighed. The last thing she wanted to do was dance with Dillon. It was hard enough pretending she wasn’t interested in him. Dancing to a slow song, feeling his body up against hers, would make it nearly impossible. Even now, just allowing him to help her up, she felt her heart beating too fast and too hard.

Sophie held herself as rigidly as she could manage, trying to put some distance between them as he drew her into his arms.

“Relax,” he murmured, pulling her closer. “I don’t bite.”

"I know that. It's just that I—I wanted to talk."

"What about?"

"Your nephew."

"Aidan?" He frowned, moving back a little. "What about him?"

"It appears he and my sister, Joy, have been seeing each other."

"Is that a problem?"

"Actually, it is."

"Why?" Another frown and he seemed to hesitate before speaking. "He's not a bad kid."

Something about his lukewarm response told Sophie that Dillon had his own reservations. "That may be," she said carefully, "but he's a senior and Joy is only a sophomore. He's too old for her."

Dillon drew her imperceptibly closer. "Like I was too old for you?" he whispered in her ear.

Sophie's entire body reacted. To disguise

what she was feeling, she immediately pulled away from him. If it wouldn't have called unwanted attention to them, she would have marched straight off the floor, forcing him to follow her if he wanted to continue the conversation. "You *were* too old for me. But that's not the point. Joy is very vulnerable. She's lost her parents, Dillon. She doesn't need any more loss in her life."

"Aidan's just as vulnerable," he said. "He's also lost his parents. And he's having a hard time adjusting to life here in Crandall Lake. At least Joy is still living in her hometown. Aidan had to give up everything. Can't you cut him a break?"

Sophie's tender heart wanted to relent, because she *did* feel bad for the boy. "I wish I could, but Joy's welfare is my top priority, and I think she'd be much better off if she and Aidan are not permitted to date."

"You sure you're not projecting what happened with us onto your sister?"

Sophie stiffened. Of course she was. How could she *not* be affected by her own mistakes? "Our situation has nothing to do with my decision regarding Joy. She and I had an agreement about her not dating older boys since she reached dating age."

"Okay, okay. I get it. And I don't want to argue with you." Now he pulled her closer still, murmuring into her ear, "I always did like dancing with you."

Thankfully, at that moment, the music stopped, and Sophie could pull away and leave the dance floor without making a scene. But as she and Dillon approached their table, she saw that Joy and Aidan were also heading in their direction.

"Sophie!" Joy called. "Wait up."

Sophie stopped, and so did Dillon. Although

Sophie's mind was churning, she couldn't help feeling a surge of pride over how pretty Joy looked in her blue dress that matched the school colors of blue and gold in her corsage. And even though Sophie was totally against Joy having any ongoing relationship with Dillon's nephew, she had to admit, if only to herself, that Joy and Aidan made a really cute couple. Aidan was tall like his uncle and had the same striking blue eyes. His hair was lighter, though, and Sophie figured the brown/gold color came from his mother. As the two kids came closer, Sophie saw the look of uncertainty on Aidan's face, and once again, she felt an unwanted sympathy for the young man.

"Sophie, I wanted you to meet Aidan," Joy said, giving Dillon a shy smile before pulling Aidan forward.

As Sophie shook the boy's hand, she was acutely aware of Dillon beside her, of Nicole

Blanchard staring at them, and probably giving her the evil eye, and most of all, of the naked longing in Joy's eyes and the tense set of Aidan's shoulders.

In that moment, Sophie knew, without a doubt, that her worst fears were true. Joy and Aidan's relationship had gone a lot further than Joy had let on. The question was, how far, and was it too late for Sophie to do anything about it?

Aidan hadn't wanted to come over to meet Sophie. But Joy had talked him into it, saying she was sure once Sophie knew him, her objections to their dating would vanish.

"I don't want to keep sneaking around," Joy told him. "I hate lying to her."

"Then don't," Aidan had answered.

"Maybe you can get away with that with your uncle, but I can't. Anyway, it makes me feel awful to lie to her. She's my *sister*, Aidan. She's all I've got. And…she's been good to me." She'd swallowed. "Please? For me?"

So here they stood, and Joy tried to telegraph, with her eyes, how much she wanted Sophie to like Aidan. She wasn't sure what she'd do if Sophie continued to forbid her to see him. She couldn't give Aidan up. She *loved* him. It was as simple as that. Sophie might think someone Joy's age couldn't possibly know what love was, but she was wrong. Maybe she'd never been in love when she was in high school, but that didn't mean it wasn't possible.

I'm going to marry Aidan someday.

"I haven't seen you dancing tonight," Dillon said.

Aidan shrugged. "I'm not very good at it."

"I'm not, either. Doesn't stop me," Dillon persisted. "You need to try new things."

Joy wished Aidan's uncle would stop criticizing Aidan. She knew he hated it. He'd told her Dillon thought he knew everything because he'd been a "hotshot" quarterback. Aidan shrugged again, then turned to Sophie. "Nice meeting you, Ms. Marlowe." Ignoring his uncle, he said, "Let's go get something to drink, Joy."

Joy looked at Sophie. On her sister's face she saw empathy, but she also saw something else. Concern. Joy knew immediately that Sophie's mind hadn't changed. Joy's heart sank, and it was all she could do to keep a smile on her face and say a nonchalant "See you later" as she and Aidan walked away.

"I hate him," Aidan muttered.

"Oh, Aidan, don't say that."

"Why not? It's true. I wish—" Abruptly, he cut off whatever he'd been going to say.

Joy sighed as they approached the drink

table. She knew what Aidan wished. He wished he could turn the clock back. He wished his parents were still alive. That he hadn't had to move to a place where he knew no one and didn't feel as if he belonged. And yet she knew he cared about *her*, that he was happy when *they* were together. She squeezed his hand to let him know she understood.

He glanced down. Grimaced. "Sorry. I didn't mean..."

"I know."

While he was getting their drinks, Joy made a vow. No matter what Sophie said, no matter what rules she tried to implement, no matter what anyone else thought, nothing and no one was going to stop her from being with Aidan.

We belong together. And that's that.

Dillon stared after the kids. *Damn.* He knew, without anyone telling him, that Aidan and

Sophie's sister, Joy, were past the point of casual dating. Maybe Sophie hadn't seen it or sensed it, but Dillon knew, just from their body language that those two kids were together in every sense of the word. Probably looking for every opportunity to be together, the way he and Sophie used to do. He smothered a sigh. *Sophie.* If not for her and what she'd said to him earlier, Dillon probably wouldn't have cared what the kids did. In fact, he might have been glad, because maybe having someone like the very pretty Joy as his girlfriend would have gone a long way toward making his nephew happier to be in Crandall Lake. And anything that made Aidan happier and easier to handle made Dillon happier.

But how could he be happy when he knew how Sophie felt? Sure enough, when his glance met hers again as they were sitting back down at their table, he saw the worry in her eyes and the way she kept looking in the direction Aidan and Joy had gone.

He reached over and squeezed her hand under the table, then leaned toward her and said softly, "Don't worry. I'll talk to Aidan. See what I can do."

Her eyes met his again. "You promise?"

He nodded.

"Thank you."

He wished they were alone somewhere. He wished he could tell her how things were with Aidan. How even if he did talk to Aidan, he doubted it would do any good. But how could he? They *weren't* alone. And even if they had been, he wasn't sure he wanted to confess that he was doing a piss-poor job of being a parent-replacement for his nephew. Hell, being with Sophie again, even as briefly as they'd been the other day and tonight, made him more self-conscience of his image than ever before. Even more so than when he was in front of millions of fans. The last thing he wanted was for her to see him in anything but a favorable light.

That realization didn't even surprise him.

Hadn't he known, the minute he'd looked into those gorgeous eyes of hers on Wednesday, that whatever it was that had drawn him to her when they were kids was even stronger now that they were adults? And that he seemed to be just as powerless to resist it as he had been then?

Sophie had a hard time falling asleep, and when she finally did, she dreamed of Dillon. The first time he ever spoke to her had been at the end of a pep rally the afternoon of a big game against Eagle Hills. She'd been a cheerleader and was wearing her uniform. He'd grinned at her as he passed on his way to the locker room.

All he'd said was, "Lookin' good, Marlowe," but those three words had told her he not only knew who she was but had remembered her name. Her heart had done crazy leapfrog things as she watched him walk away. He was the cutest, coolest, sexiest boy she'd ever seen.

That night, at the community center—there was always a dance on Friday and Saturday nights—he'd asked her to dance. She'd nearly fainted with delight as he took her hand and pulled her into his arms. And when he'd whispered in her ear that he'd like to take her home, she wasn't sure she could walk off the dance floor without help.

They'd gone to the lake afterward. That was where all the kids went to make out. When he'd kissed her, Sophie's head felt as if it was going to explode. And when his hand had moved from her waist to her breast, she very nearly *did* faint. Every nerve in her body came alive, and from that moment on, she was his.

The next morning, memories of her dream lingering, she knew her sister wasn't the only one in this house who was in danger of making a monumental mistake. She also knew she couldn't put off talking to Joy. Trouble was, Sophie hated confrontation.

She wished Beth, who'd been her BFF since they were kindergartners together, was home so she could run all this by her first. But Beth was on her honeymoon in Italy, and Sophie had vowed she would not yield to the temptation of calling Beth unless blood was involved.

"Don't be ridiculous," Beth had said when Sophie made the promise as they hugged goodbye after Beth had tossed her wedding bouquet. "You can call or text. Mark won't mind."

But Sophie knew Mark *would* mind, and Sophie didn't blame him. A honeymoon should be sacred. No man wanted his new bride thinking about anyone other than *him*. Time enough for real life when the newlyweds got back home.

No, Sophie was on her own. And since there was no one else she trusted enough to confide in, she would have to handle this problem with Joy by herself.

And I can't put it off, either. Sighing, she got up from the kitchen table where she'd been drinking coffee and reading the news on her iPad. It was almost ten, and Joy was still asleep. Sophie had heard her sister come in at one o'clock the night before, right on time for her curfew, which Sophie had extended for the homecoming dance.

Deciding Joy had slept long enough, Sophie walked upstairs and softly knocked at Joy's bedroom door. When there was no acknowledgment, Sophie knocked harder. Still hearing nothing, she opened the door and peered in. "Joy? Time to get up."

"Huh? Wha? Wh-what time is it?"

"After ten."

"Wh-why do I have to get up?" Joy pulled the cotton coverlet she used over her head.

Normally Sophie would have relented, because Joy was good about getting up on time and rarely gave Sophie problems in the morning, so Sophie gave her some slack on the weekends. But today wasn't a normal day, at least not in Sophie's mind. Today was the day she had to take whatever steps necessary to ensure that Joy did nothing stupid, nothing that would get in the way of the future she deserved, and more important, nothing that would break her heart down the line.

"We need to talk," Sophie said firmly, walking over to the bed and sitting down next to Joy. "Get up and wash your face and do whatever else you need to do, then come downstairs and have some breakfast and we'll talk, okay?"

Joy just looked at her. And from the expression on her face, Sophie knew Joy had a pretty good idea of what the subject of their talk would be. Sophie also knew Joy wanted to protest, but to her credit, she only sighed.

"Okay," she said.

Sophie's heart melted a little as she gazed down at the sister she loved so much, the sister who almost felt like her daughter. But even as she wanted to lean over and kiss Joy's cheek and say not to worry, she knew she couldn't give in to the understanding and sympathy she felt. *It's for her own good. She'll thank me someday.* Sophie squeezed Joy's shoulder and got up. "Would you like to have pancakes today?" she said brightly.

"Sure," Joy said.

"All right. See you downstairs."

Fifteen minutes later, barefoot and dressed in denim cutoffs and a faded One Direction T-shirt, her long blond hair pulled back into a ponytail, Joy entered the kitchen. Opening the refrigerator, she took out the carton of skim milk and poured herself a glass. She drank it leaning against the kitchen counter.

Sophie smiled at her and ladled batter into the frying pan. She'd already put syrup and butter on the table. "Want to put two plates out?"

"Sure."

It only took a couple of minutes for the first batch of pancakes to be ready. Sophie put them on a waiting platter, covered it with foil to keep the pancakes warm, then put a second batch on to cook. Once there were enough pancakes to feed both of them, she turned off the stove, moved the hot frying pan to a cool burner and joined her sister at the table.

Since it was obvious Joy wasn't going to ask any questions about what Sophie might want to talk about, Sophie waited until they'd both eaten a couple of pancakes before saying, "I'm glad I got a chance to meet Aidan last night."

Joy, who had been hunched over her plate, looked up. Sophie's heart pinched at the hopeful light in the girl's eyes.

"I told you he was nice," Joy said.

"He does seem very nice."

"So it's okay if I date him."

"That's not what I said." Earlier Sophie had fixed herself another cup of coffee and she drank some.

"Why *not*, if you like him?"

Sophie sighed. "Joy, you know why not. He's too old for you. That fact didn't magically change because I met him and he seems like a nice boy. He's still too old." *And troubled.*

Myriad emotions played across Joy's face. "That's not *fair*!"

Sophie wished she could tell Joy she understood perfectly, that she'd felt exactly the same way when she was Joy's age and wildly in love with Dillon. Could she? She wouldn't have to tell Joy *who* the boy had been, but she could share some of what she'd gone through.

Tears welled in Joy's eyes as they stared at each other. Sophie battled the desire to comfort her, to give in, to make her sister happy. "I know you don't think I understand, but I do. You have to trust me on this. You're too young to be seriously dating to begin with, and Aidan *is* too old for you. Honey, he'll be going off to college next year. And then what?"

Sophie reached across the table to take Joy's hand, but Joy snatched it away. She pushed her chair back. Her face looked like thunder-clouds. "He's less than two years older than me! You're just using his age as an excuse because you think you know everything and I don't know *anything*! So what if he's going away to college next year? What difference does *that* make? He's here *now*! And…and I really like him. And he likes me! I—I can't wait till I'm eighteen and I can make my *own* decisions!"

"Joy…"

"Sometimes I *hate* you!"

And before Sophie could say another word, Joy had jumped up and run from the room. Sophie sank back in her chair and listened to

Joy pounding up the stairs, followed by the sound of her bedroom door slamming shut.

"Well, *that* went well," Sophie muttered as she debated what to do. Should she go after Joy? Maybe tell her about Dillon and what had happened between them? Without mentioning any names, of course. She thought back to the heartbreak she'd felt when Dillon left Crandall Lake…and her…and gone off to college. She'd cried for days, weeks. She hadn't wanted to go anywhere or do anything. She'd haunted the mailbox, thinking Dillon would surely *write* to her. But he didn't. She'd almost broken down and called him, but at the last minute she came to her senses and ignored the urge. It took her a long time to regain some kind of normality, because for months she'd felt as if the world were crashing down on her. Which was probably exactly the way her sister felt right now.

Sophie sighed for probably the tenth time that morning.

Would it do any good to tell Joy any of this?

Would it have stopped you from seeing Dillon if Mom had warned you off him? Sophie's mother hadn't because she'd been too preoccupied with a new husband, a three-year-old Joy and a full-time job as an office manager.

But even if she *had* realized what was going on with Sophie and Dillon and said something, Sophie had to be honest with herself. It wouldn't have made a difference. Nothing in the world would have kept Sophie away from Dillon. Certainly not what some adult had said. When you fall in love with someone the way Sophie had fallen in love with Dillon, nothing *anyone* said would have mattered.

Face it. It's obvious things have progressed with Joy and Aidan to the point where she won't hear you. She'll continue to sneak around and see Aidan the way she's been doing.

Sophie sighed again as she got up from the table and cleared the breakfast remains. The only thing she could do now was make sure that when Joy *did* see Aidan, she saw him here at the house, where Sophie had some control over what they did.

Sophie knew her plan was a Band-Aid when what she needed was major surgery, but until she came up with something better, it would have to do.

Chapter Four

As Halloween approached, the weather had finally begun to feel like autumn, with cool nights and mild days. In this part of Texas, the leaves hadn't yet turned—that wouldn't happen for another month or so—but it still *felt* like fall.

Normally Joy loved this time of year. But the atmosphere at home—the way Sophie constantly watched her—had taken some of the pleasure out of it. And yet how could Joy complain? Sophie, for some mysterious reason Joy couldn't fathom, had relented and Joy was at least allowed to *see* Aidan. Sophie had consented to him coming over twice a week, just as long as she was there and Joy and Aidan did not go upstairs to Joy's bedroom, which limited them to the living room or dining room that had been converted into an art studio for Joy. Sophie watched them so closely that they hadn't been able to make love more than twice that month, and both times had been hurried affairs—once in his car and once at school, in a storage closet near the gym—where Joy had been terrified of being caught.

But there was something else nagging at Joy. Something she'd been trying to ignore. Something she'd been pretending didn't exist—the undeniable fact that she'd missed two periods. Since she was twelve and had begun her menstrual cycle, she'd been pretty much like clockwork. Every twenty-seven days her period started and it lasted five days. Joy kept track on her iPhone calendar.

Joy told herself she wasn't actually worried. Not really. Aidan always used condoms, so there was no way she could be pregnant. Well, he had almost always used them. There was that one time they did it in the pool, early in the morning, when no one else was there.

Her face heated as she thought about how sexy that was, how he'd been all upset about something and come to seek her out before the pool opened and found her alone setting everything up that morning. She'd never forget Aidan's anger and frustration toward his uncle and how he'd started kissing her and how, underwater, he'd pushed her bathing suit aside and shoved himself into her. Even now, thinking about how it had felt to do it in the water, she felt all shivery and tingling down there. Because the sex was unplanned, neither of them had a condom. Neither of them even *thought* about a condom. Joy had just wanted to comfort him and make him feel better.

And then, once it had happened, it was so wonderful she wished they never had to use condoms again. She'd even thought about getting on the pill, but that would have meant asking Sophie, because Joy couldn't imagine how she could do it without Sophie's knowledge and permission. Not in a town as small as Crandall Lake. And certainly not if she wanted to keep living with Sophie.

When had the pool sex happened? Joy bit her bottom lip and thought back. It wasn't in June, because she'd only met Aidan in June. July. It was in July, after the Fourth, but before Aidan's birthday on the twentieth, when he'd turned eighteen.

She swallowed. *Oh God.* Could she be pregnant? She closed her eyes, and her heart thudded. No. No. God wouldn't do that to her, would He?

"Senorita Ferrelli. Senorita *Ferrelli*!"

Joy's eyes flew open, and she nearly jumped out of her seat.

"If you're bored with this class, maybe you'd rather go visit the principal's office instead." The speaker was Mrs. Perez, the Spanish teacher. Her dark eyes, normally friendly, pinned Joy.

"Lo siento, señora."

Mrs. Perez nodded, but she gave Joy a thoughtful look, almost as if she knew *exactly* what Joy had been thinking about.

For the rest of the class, Joy tried hard to concentrate because she really liked Mrs. Perez *and* she liked Spanish, but that thought… that frightening thought…that *unbelievable* thought…that maybe…just maybe…the one time she and Aidan had had unprotected sex had left her pregnant…would not go away.

Dillon had spent the ten days after homecoming working hard with the team, juggling the problems that came with a season where they were neither winning nor losing, but some of both, dealing as best he could with his defiant and still-resentful and unhappy nephew, and trying to forget about Sophie—sexy, beautiful, intelligent Sophie—who seemed to have taken up permanent residence in his mind, whether he wanted her there or not.

He told himself the last thing he needed was a complicated relationship, and it *would* be complicated, especially considering the kind of woman Sophie was at heart—the marriage, picket-fence kind—and the situation between her sister and Aidan, a situation Sophie didn't approve of. He also told himself he wasn't planning to settle permanently in Crandall Lake. He was only here temporarily to see if he liked it. Maybe he would decide he didn't want to stay here for the rest of his life. Maybe he would eventually decide he wouldn't mind being a sportscaster or play-by-play analyst the way his former agent kept encouraging him to be, and once Aiden was off to school, he would leave this place and never look back.

So…no.

Sophie was not for him.

Who cared if those plump lips of hers just begged to be kissed? Who cared that her curves still had the power to cause him to squirm? Who cared if he couldn't seem to banish her from his mind…or his dreams?

Because he *was* dreaming of her. The other night he'd relived the first time they'd met and the first time they'd made love. It had been so real he was unable to shake the feeling that his subconscious was trying to tell him something.

No.

He couldn't go there.

He had to forget about her.

There were plenty of other sexy, beautiful and intelligent women out there. He did not have to get entangled with someone who would only cause him grief. He could do this. He could forget about Sophie. It was mind over matter, just as everything was.

Decision made.

He would shove sexy Sophie out of his mind.

Permanently.

Sophie was so busy with her job and worrying about Joy that she didn't have a lot of time to think about anything else, but even so, after that dream she'd had, when she wasn't on guard, thoughts of Dillon managed to creep into her mind. It didn't help that she seemed to see him at least once a day. Or that the other single women who worked at the school seemed to talk about him constantly.

Even Beth, who should know better, brought up his name fairly regularly. That morning was a perfect example.

Ran into D. at Packers, she texted.

Sophie was on her way to school, so she didn't answer until she'd parked in the parking lot. Why R U telling me this?

U care. U know U do.

Go bother somebody else.

OK. But U know U want to know what he said.

I do not!

Liar!!!!!!!!!!!!!

By then, Sophie had reached her classroom, so she turned the sound off her cell, slipped it into her purse and told herself she had no interest in what Dillon and Beth had talked about.

But the whole subject had nagged at her all morning. And now here it was, afternoon, and she was on her way home, and it was *still* nagging at her. Had they talked about *her*? She would kill Beth if she'd said anything.

She thought about how Beth had somehow managed to drag out of her how she'd felt when they were dancing the night of homecoming.

"You still care about him, don't you?"

Sophie wanted to say no, but she couldn't seem to get the word out.

"I *knew* it. I just knew it."

"What do you mean, you *knew* it?" After those first few months when she was so devastated by his leaving, Sophie had never talked about Dillon. Not once. She pretended to everyone that she'd always expected him to go and it didn't bother her at all. And she'd done a good job of it. After all, she had her pride. Especially since she'd known the situation was hopeless and that Dillon was never coming back. Yes, she'd covered her tracks well. So no way Beth knew anything.

"Because I know you well enough to know when you're avoiding a subject, Sophie."

"It's true I don't want to talk about him. He's an old subject, Beth. I've moved on."

But Beth hadn't seemed convinced, and obviously from her text earlier, she still wasn't.

Sophie sighed. She had to stop thinking about Dillon. If she didn't, Beth was going to continue to hound her, because she seemed to have a sixth sense where Sophie and Dillon were concerned. And what *had* those two talked about yesterday?

She was still lecturing herself on the subject as she arrived home and walked in the front door. But all thoughts of Beth and Dillon and what they might or might not have said about her disappeared from her mind the moment she saw Joy, who was sitting on the couch in the living room and staring into space. Every inch of her body looked forlorn. And when she turned her head at Sophie's entrance, Sophie saw that Joy's eyes were puffy and red from crying.

Sophie's heart practically stopped. *Ohmigod.* What had happened? She started to form the words, but before she could get even one word out, Joy jumped up and practically flew into Sophie's arms. Fresh tears soaked Sophie's white blouse and Sophie could feel her sister's body trembling.

"Joy, honey, what's wrong?"

"I—I—I… Oh, Sophie!" Joy wailed.

"What? Joy, you're scaring me." Sophie wanted to cry herself. What was it? What had happened? Had someone died?

But Joy just kept crying and Sophie knew she'd have to first calm her sister before she could get the girl to talk. So she patted her back and repeated that no matter what it was, everything would be okay. Finally, after what seemed like an hour or more, but was probably only about ten minutes, Joy's sobs quieted and she drew a deep, shuddering breath and extricated herself from Sophie's arms.

"Better?" Sophie said, leading Joy back to the couch and sitting beside her. She kept hold of Joy's hand and added softly, "Tell me."

Joy took another deep breath and her eyes—her beautiful blue eyes met Sophie's. "I—I'm pregnant."

Those two words struck Sophie like an arrow through the heart. They were the last two words she would ever have imagined coming from Joy's mouth. And yet, as their eyes continued to stay locked together, as the words sank in, as quiet seconds passed with only the sound of someone's lawn mower going in the distance, Sophie realized that this news wasn't really the shock she'd first thought it would be.

Hadn't she always had this secret fear?

She'd had this same fear for *herself* years ago, but she'd been lucky.

Oh, Joy.

"What am I going to do?" Joy whispered. "I—I'm so sorry, Sophie."

Sophie took a deep breath of her own. She had known similar situations quite a few times in her years at the high school. Anger would do no good…for anyone…at least not for anyone in this room.

"How do you know you're pregnant? Have you seen a doctor?" She frowned, glancing at Joy's belly. "You don't look a bit different." But was that true? Now that she really looked, Sophie could see that Joy did look as if she'd gained a little weight, but not so much that it was noticeable. "How far along are you? Do you know?"

"I—I haven't seen a doctor, but I did three of those tests. You know, the ones you pee on? And they all turned positive."

Sophie wanted to cry. So many thoughts tumbled through her mind. A baby. How in the world could Joy have a baby? She was only *sixteen*! And yet what was the alternative? Sophie knew that Joy would never want to have an abortion. The truth was, Sophie couldn't bear the thought herself.

"Does…does Aidan know? I'm assuming Aidan *is* the father?"

Joy looked stricken at the question. "Of course he's the father. I've never been with anyone else."

"I'm sorry. I didn't mean that. I just…I'm having a hard time processing this."

Joy ducked her head. "I know."

Sophie sighed. She put her arm around Joy's shoulders, felt the trembling. "Let's go out to the kitchen. There's some iced tea in the fridge. Let's be comfortable and…talk about this."

Once they were seated across the table from each other, glasses of iced tea in front of them, Joy said, "You asked if Aidan knows. No. I haven't told him yet. I—I just figured it out today. And I was so upset I couldn't even think of talking to him."

Sophie nodded. "When you do, what do you think he'll say?"

Joy shook her head. "I don't know. He... he'll be upset. I mean, why wouldn't he be? He's planning to go to college next year. Ohio State." Joy met Sophie's eyes. "All he's talked about is going back to Ohio and starting college where his parents both went to school."

Left unsaid but obviously something Joy was thinking about, just as Sophie was, was the fact that before meeting Aidan, all Joy could talk about was going to a school like the Rhode Island School of Design or the Art Institute of Chicago. It hurt Sophie to even *think* that Joy might not be able to go to *any* school. She was so talented and had such a bright future ahead of her. *Oh God, this was such a mess.*

Sophie drank some of her tea to give herself more time to think. Finally she said, "You know, a pregnancy doesn't have to mean the end of the world. We can figure something out."

Joy grimaced. "Like what? Pretty soon I'm going to be as big as a house and everyone's going to know. Oh God. I wish I was dead."

"Honey, don't say that. Don't ever say that."

"Well, I do!" Joy's eyes filled with tears again. "I might as well be. Aidan will hate me when he finds out. And everyone will be talking about me, and the boys will all be snickering and saying things."

"Aidan doesn't have any right to hate you," Sophie said. "You didn't do this on your own, you know." Now she was mad. Dammit. Dillon had said he'd talk to his nephew, and it was obvious he hadn't. Well, she'd have a few choice words…for both of them.

"You…you don't think we should get married, do you?" Joy said.

"Good grief, no! You don't *want* to get married, do you?"

Joy shook her head, dejection written all over her. "I—I do love him, but…I—I don't know. I want to go to school, and…and we're too young to get married, aren't we? He wouldn't want to anyway."

Sophie knew, just by the pain in Joy's eyes, that she wasn't certain about Aidan's feelings for her. The poor kid. Sophie felt like crying herself. But she knew it was time to put on her big-girl panties and counsel Joy the way she would counsel any young woman in this predicament. "Look, if I were counseling someone else in your shoes, my advice would be to decide how she wanted to proceed before she told the boy in question. So don't worry about what Aidan will think or want. Decide what *you* think and *you* want."

"I want this not to have happened," Joy said.

"Yes, I know, but it *has* happened."

"Maybe I could go away somewhere?" Joy said hopefully. "Have the baby and give it up for adoption?"

"That's definitely an option."

"But what would we *say*? I mean, people would ask questions, and then they'd *know*, wouldn't they?"

"Maybe not." But Sophie knew Joy was probably right. What story could they possibly tell that would convince anyone about anything? She couldn't help thinking about Kaitlyn Lowe, the senior Sophie had counseled last month. Kaitlyn's parents had said Kaitlyn was going to spend the remainder of the year with her grandparents in New Jersey because her grandmother was failing and Kaitlyn was her only granddaughter, but tongues had wagged. Crandall Lake was a small town. People generally knew everything there was to know in small towns. And no one had swallowed that story.

For long moments, the sisters sat thinking about what they'd just discussed; then Joy heaved a sigh. "I know two things. I don't want to have the baby and raise it myself. And I don't want to have an abortion. So I think the best thing is giving it up for adoption."

Sophie nodded slowly. That did seem like the best option.

"I guess I should call Aidan, then," Joy said. "Talk to him."

"Go ahead. Go for a drive somewhere. See what he has to say. Then tomorrow we'll decide where we go from here."

And in the meantime, she thought, while Joy and Aidan were off somewhere talking, she would go over to Dillon's house and do some talking of her own.

* * *

Dillon looked shocked when he saw her on his doorstep.

"Hey, Sophie." He frowned when he saw the expression on her face. "Something wrong?"

"You could say that."

"What is it?"

"We need to talk."

"Okay. C'mon in." He stood aside as she entered the house. "Let's go into the den. Can I get you something to drink?"

"No, thanks. I don't plan to stay long." Ignoring his gesture to follow him into the den, she added, "What I have to say can be said in a few words. Your nephew, Aidan, has gotten my sister, Joy, pregnant."

Dillon stared at her. "Say what?"

"You heard me."

"Jesus, Mary and Joseph."

"They aren't going to help you."

He continued to stare at her. "Are you sure?"

"What? That Joy is pregnant? Or that Aidan is the father? I'm sure of both, and I'm also sure that your nephew was irresponsible and took advantage of Joy, who, as you know, is a good bit younger and a lot less experienced than I'm sure *he* is. So don't even think about encouraging him to weasel out of this, or trying to talk Joy into getting an abortion, because neither she nor I am willing to even entertain the idea."

He held his hands up as if to ward off a blow. "Hey, hey, slow down."

But Sophie was just getting started. "Joy wants to go away and have the baby and give it up for adoption, and as far as I'm concerned, if we can figure out how to do this, you and he can just plan on paying her expenses for everything involved."

"Jeez, Sophie, give a guy a break, will ya?"

"What do you mean?"

"I mean, quit making assumptions and quit accusing me of things I hadn't even thought of saying."

"Oh, don't go giving me that innocent act, Dillon. I'm sure your nephew knows the kind of life you've led the past ten years or so. You've set a certain example and he's just following in your footsteps." She glared at him. "Tell me. How many babies have *you* left behind?"

His eyes were like daggers. "You don't think much of me, do you?"

"If the shoe fits..."

Now he looked as if he'd like to shake her. In fact, the expression on his face frightened her enough that she backed up.

For a long moment, he just looked at her.

Sophie tried to stay angry, because she knew once she let go of the anger and allowed herself to really *think* about the dilemma Joy was in, she might give in to the temptation to throw herself into his arms. She bit her lip. She could feel tears threatening. Suddenly the whole thing seemed overwhelming, and she had a much better understanding of the ways the parents of the girls she'd counseled in the past had felt. Why? Why had this happened? Her eyes met Dillon's, and she swallowed.

"Ah, Sophie," he said softly, reaching for her. "I'm sorry."

At that moment, Sophie knew she was lost. And when he drew her into his arms, she didn't even try to resist. Melting against him, she raised her face and gave herself up to the comfort of his kiss.

But the kiss that started as something soft and sweet quickly became more and more demanding, filled with a hunger that quickly raged out of control. Sophie's heart thundered, her head spun, every sense came alive as if it had been hibernating for years and only waiting for this moment and this man and everything he had always made her feel. As Dillon's tongue delved and his hands roamed, heating every inch they touched, Sophie moaned. Every cell in her body wanted more, *had* to have more. When he swept her up and into his arms, still kissing her, she didn't protest. She didn't even think of stopping him.

"Are you sure?" he asked, his voice raspy, his eyes glazed with desire as they studied her face.

"Yes," she whispered. "Yes."

Moments later, in his first-floor bedroom with the door shut, they lay tangled on his bed. Soon kissing and touching through their clothes wasn't enough, and they frantically began undressing each other.

Sophie's breath caught at the sight of him.

Was there anything as glorious to look at as a gorgeous, naked man—a man you've always loved—even if you've been unable to admit it until now?

"You're so beautiful," he murmured as he stroked her skin, then kissed his way down her body. "So beautiful."

Sophie arched her back, giving herself up to the sensations and emotions pummeling her. She grasped his hair in both fists as his mouth tasted and found her sweet spot, barely breathing as an almost unbearable tension built, pushing her higher and higher until she exploded in wave after wave of exquisite pleasure that shuddered through her and left her shaking and weak.

But not so weak she didn't want more. Reaching for him, she found him hard and hot and ready. Now it was his turn to groan as she guided him inside. She gasped as she felt him fill her, his heat causing that delicious tension to build again, rising to a crescendo as he thrust again and again until he erupted. Tightening her legs around him, she held him close as he shook and gasped. Her own body felt on fire, as if it were lit from within, as if she was in the only place in the world she had ever belonged.

They lay together, their hearts slowing, their bodies cooling, for a long time. Finally he stirred, lifting his head and looking down at her.

"Are you sorry?" he whispered. His eyes were tender as they studied her.

"No." But she would be tomorrow. She probably would be five minutes from now, when she'd had time to reflect on just exactly what she'd done.

"I'm not, either." He rolled off her, pulling her close against him. He brushed her hair away from her face and kissed her softly, his lips lingering against hers. "I've wanted you from the moment I saw you in the hallway at school that day."

Sophie swallowed. She'd wanted him, too. "We never *could* stay away from each other," she said wryly.

"So, what do we do now?"

"About what? Us? Or the kids?"

He smiled crookedly. "Both."

"Well," she said, sighing, "right now I don't know. I do know Joy is too young to be a mother, and she knows it, too. And I'm sure you feel the same way about Aidan."

"Frankly, I can't imagine him with a kid. Hell, he can barely handle his life as it is, let alone adding a kid to the mix."

Sophie sighed again. "Joy's with him now."

"Telling him?"

"Yes."

"I feel sorry for them both."

"I do, too." After thinking for a moment, she said, "Tell you what. Let's wait and see how they feel after they talk. You talk to Aidan tonight and I'll talk to Joy. And maybe tomorrow, all four of us can get together and come up with a plan." Adding, "Now I think I'd better go," Sophie started to extricate herself from his arms, but he stopped her.

"We won't let the kids' situation make a difference to us, will we?"

"I don't know, Dillon. I—I'll have to sleep on that, too."

"I understand," he said. "I just want you to know it doesn't make a difference to *me*."

As Sophie drove home, his words haunted her. They were nice words, yes, but there were other words he *hadn't* said. Words like *I love you* and *We belong together.* Sure, he wanted sex, but Sophie wanted more. She always had.

The question was, was Dillon finally prepared to give it to her?

Or would this renewal of their desire for each other end exactly the same way it did the first time?

Chapter Five

Dillon sat nursing a beer while waiting for Aidan to come in. He still wasn't sure what he'd say to the boy, but he knew he couldn't put off this conversation. Not after what Sophie had revealed. And especially not after what had then happened between him and Sophie.

Dillon wasn't the particularly reflective type, especially when it came to sex. The favors of beautiful women had been freely offered ever since his college glory days and he'd rarely looked back or regretted his actions. He'd figured all parties were consenting adults and had enjoyed the experience.

But Sophie was different.

Very different.

And truth be told, Dillon felt differently *about* her.

So he knew he had to tread carefully. Especially if he wanted their relationship to continue.

Did he?

With his thoughts running in this vein, he didn't realize Aidan was home until he heard the front door open. Before the kid could escape to his bedroom upstairs, Dillon got up and walked out into the hall. "Hey," he said.

Aidan turned around.

Dillon wasn't surprised to see how drawn the boy looked. Drawn and worried and…

scared. Well, that was understandable. If, at eighteen, Dillon had found himself in the predicament Aidan now found himself in, he'd have been scared out of his mind. And even though Aidan wasn't a sports star and looking at a full scholarship as Dillon had been, he was an intelligent young man with a bright future ahead of him. A future that didn't include being a father before his life even got started.

"I think we need to talk," Dillon said quietly.

"I'm tired. I just want to go to bed."

"I'm sure you do, but we still need to talk."

Aidan started to protest, but Dillon cut him off. "I know what Joy told you tonight. Her sister came over to fill me in."

Aidan's face reddened. "I don't need a lecture."

"That's not what I intended. I just want to talk to you. We need to decide what to do."

"*We* don't need to do anything!"

Normally when Aidan gave him lip, Dillon got mad. Tonight all he felt was sadness. "C'mon, Aidan. Cut me a break, would you? Whether you believe it or not, I care about you. I know you're upset and you don't know what to do. So let's sit down and calmly go over your options. I can help you."

Tears sprang into Aidan's eyes, which surprised Dillon. He quickly turned away, but not quickly enough. "You don't care," he mumbled.

Was that what Aidan thought? Dillon put his arm around Aidan's shoulders. Through the stiffness, he could feel the boy trembling. "I do care," he said softly. "You're my brother's son. I love you."

Aidan swallowed, and even though Dillon

could see how he was struggling not to, he began to cry.

"C'mon, let's go out to the kitchen. Want… some hot chocolate?" He'd been about to offer the kid a beer, then realized that wasn't a smart thing to do. More to the point, it wasn't legal. Fishing in his jean's pocket, Dillon pulled out a handkerchief and handed it to the boy.

Aidan blew his nose, and although he didn't say anything, he did follow Dillon to the kitchen. While Aidan composed himself, Dillon brewed a cup of hot chocolate for his nephew, then took a fresh beer out of the fridge for himself.

"So, what did Ms. Marlowe have to say?" Aidan said, calm now. "She think I'm scum?"

Dillon shook his head. "No, but she's upset and concerned. How do *you* feel?

"How do you think I feel? I feel stupid."

"Didn't you think about using condoms or something?"

"We *did* use condoms. It was only one time we didn't." Aidan shook his head. "I can't believe that I made just *one* stupid mistake, and now she's pregnant!"

"It wasn't just your mistake," Dillon pointed out. "It takes two, y'know."

Aidan sighed heavily. "It was my fault," he mumbled.

"It doesn't really matter whose fault it is, does it? What's done is done. Now the question is what to do about it."

Aidan nodded.

"So, did the two of you talk about that tonight?"

Aidan shrugged. "Yeah, some. Joy said she thinks the best thing would be for her to go away and have the baby, then give it up for adoption."

"And what do *you* think?"

"I don't know. I guess that's best." Aidan grimaced. "I don't really want her to go away, but I can't be a *father*."

"Did Joy suggest you should be?"

"No. She…I don't think she wants to be a mother, either. I mean, she plans to go away to school, too."

"Well, then…I guess you two *have* decided."

"But…"

"But what?"

"Where will she go? She…she didn't seem to know. And who's gonna pay for her to live somewhere else and have a baby? I don't have any money. Just my college trust fund, and you said it could only be used for college."

That wasn't technically true. Dillon *had* said that, but only because he didn't want Aidan to think he could go out and buy an expensive sports car or go off to Vegas or something.

Aidan's trust fund had been set up through his parents' wills, but Dillon was its trustee and he'd considered it his duty to make sure the money left to Aidan was spent wisely so that he would still have a considerable sum left even after finishing college.

"Money won't be a problem," Dillon said carefully. "If that's what the two of you want, then it can be arranged."

"Are…are you sure?"

Dillon almost smiled at the relief in Aidan's eyes. Reaching across the table, he grasped his nephew's hand. "I'm sure."

"But what about Ms. Marlowe? Do you think she'll want Joy to go somewhere else?"

"I think she'll want whatever is best for Joy."

"Yeah, I guess. But…"

"But what?"

"I—I… I don't know what I'll do if Joy goes away."

With that admission, Dillon knew just how miserable and lonely and lost his nephew felt. Just how hard the past months had been for him. Dillon had thought he understood. After all, his parents had both been gone by the time Dillon turned thirty. But Aidan was only eighteen. He'd lost his dad when he was thirteen. And his mother at seventeen. Plus, he'd lost his home and all his friends and everything familiar in his life. He'd been forced to live with an uncle to whom he'd never been close. Move to a new town where he knew no one.

No wonder he'd turned to Joy.

"We'll figure it out," Dillon said gently.

But even as Aidan nodded agreement, his eyes remained bleak.

After his nephew had gone up to bed, Dillon remained downstairs. Jeez, Dillon thought, it was hard to grow up. And it was especially hard when you did something that had such serious and far-reaching consequences.

Sophie did not want to get up and face the day. It would have been bad enough if all she'd had to deal with was Joy's problem, but now she also had to think about the consequences of her *own* actions last night.

Why had she so been so quick to jump in the sack with Dillon? Okay, so she was upset and he'd comforted her. But sex? Hadn't she learned *anything* from their past? Dillon did not have the stick-to-it gene. He was used to taking what he wanted and making a quick exit when he was finished. And she was not that kind of woman. She couldn't have casual sex and then forget about it. She wanted something meaningful. Something lasting.

You are so stupid.

Sophie sighed deeply. Well, there was no

law that said she had to continue to be stupid, was there? She'd made a mistake, but she didn't have to repeat it.

And yet, even as she vowed to be stronger in the future, she couldn't help remembering just how wonderful the sex between her and Dillon had been. Even thinking about it made her want him again. God, she was a mess. Beth would laugh her fool head off if she knew. But she wouldn't know. No one could know. Because Sophie wasn't going to do anything even remotely similar again. Last night was an aberration. She'd been upset and Dillon had taken advantage of that.

But was that assessment fair? If Sophie was being honest, *totally* honest, she knew it wasn't. She had wanted what Dillon was offering and she'd given him no resistance at all. In fact, she'd practically invited him to make love to her. The moment he put his arms around her, she'd been like a ripe peach, ready and willing for him to take a bite.

That thought made her chuckle. Now she was even thinking in bad metaphors. Telling herself she'd better stop thinking and start getting ready for her day, she finished packing herself a lunch, found her tote bag, called a goodbye to Joy and left the house with five minutes to spare.

Joy heard the slam of the front door, which meant Sophie had left for the day. Burying her head back under the covers, Joy decided she would stay in bed for a while longer. She blessed Sophie for saying she could skip school today. There was no way she'd have been able to face Megan or her other friends or her teachers. Now that she knew her condition, it felt as if all anyone had to do was look at her and they'd know, too.

On one level Joy knew this was ridiculous. No one could possibly know. Yet no matter how many times she told herself this, she didn't totally believe it. She probably had such a guilty look on her face that they'd guess. How long would it take for them to notice her weight gain? She'd wonder what they'd all think when she suddenly moved away. Would they guess then?

And Megan. What would Megan think? Should she tell her? She didn't want to. She didn't want to tell anyone.

Last night Sophie had said that tonight she would call Mandy, their cousin, the daughter of their mother's older sister. Mandy lived in Los Angeles and worked for a big advertising agency, and Joy had always liked her a lot. In fact, she'd spent her last two spring breaks visiting Mandy. Mandy was twenty-six and really, really cool. Sophie said she thought Mandy would agree to having Joy come and spend the rest of her pregnancy in LA. Mandy had once suggested that when Joy turned eighteen she might spend summers interning at Mandy's agency. Perhaps that internship was still an option.

Part of Joy felt nothing but relief at the thought of living with Mandy. But the other part, the part that loved Aidan so much, felt sick at heart. How would she bear being so far away from him? Yet when she told him her idea of going away to have their baby, he hadn't said a word in protest. Remembering the flare of hope on his face made tears spring to her eyes.

He'd been glad! He didn't care that she might go away. That possibly they wouldn't see each other again. That their baby, the one they'd made together, would go to some stranger.

For the rest of the morning, Joy cried out

her desolation and disappointment. But by the time Sophie returned home that afternoon, Joy was resigned.

What was done was done.

And if going away for the rest of the school year and giving away her baby was the price she would have to pay for her sins, she had no right to complain.

Dillon knew he couldn't talk to Sophie at school, so he waited until he got home before calling her. "I talked to Aidan last night."

"And?"

"And he said he and Joy had discussed her going away, having the baby and giving it up for adoption. He said that's what she wanted to do."

"Yes, both she and I have decided that's the best solution."

"He's worried about where she'll go, though.

And he and I both wanted you to know we'll pay all of her expenses."

"That's generous of you, Dillon. There won't be a lot. I plan to ask my cousin in LA to let Joy stay with her until after the baby comes."

"What'll you tell people?"

"That she has an opportunity to join a work/study program for artists sponsored by UCLA and it'll give her a tremendous heads-up for college. I'll hint that she will probably stay out there permanently."

"You've really thought about this, huh?" For some reason, Sophie's reasonableness bothered him. Shouldn't she be more upset? Hell, *he* was.

"I've thought about nothing else for most of the night."

He'd thought about nothing but *her* for most of the night. But immediately Dillon was ashamed of himself...and the thought. There were much more pressing issues at hand. Still, he couldn't stop himself from saying, "Sophie, once this is settled, I want to see you again."

"I don't think this is the right time to talk about that," she answered stiffly.

Oh, hell. He shouldn't have said that. What was wrong with him? He sounded insensitive. "I know. I just...I wanted you to know how I feel."

"I'd better go. I want to call Mandy. Get everything settled."

"Will you let me know if everything's okay after you talk to her?"

"I don't think—" Abruptly, she stopped. "All right. Sure."

"Thanks."

After they hung up, Dillon thought about the conversation for a long time before heading toward the kitchen, where he planned to make a pot of chili for his and Aidan's dinner. He guessed there was no reason for him to feel disappointed by Sophie's less-than-enthusiastic reaction to his declaration. She'd been right. He'd picked a bad time to tell her how he felt. All she cared about right now was making sure everything was set up for Joy and the baby.

Time enough to think about the direction he and Sophie might be headed. Besides, why had he said *anything* to her when he'd already decided it would probably be best not to see her again at all?

Because you're thinking with the wrong part of your anatomy, that's why. From now on, use your brain.

"Oh, Sophie, I would've liked nothing better, but it'll be impossible for Joy to come out here to stay with me. My company is sending me to Europe for the next eight or nine months, maybe longer."

Sophie wanted to cry. "Really? When did this happen?"

"Just yesterday. In fact, I had you on the top of my list to call."

"Wh-what will you do in Europe? I didn't think you had an office there."

"We don't. That's the point. But if we're going to compete in the international market-place, we need to have one. That's going to be my responsibility. Open an office in London, and then—if all goes well—they mentioned possibly sending me to Sydney after that."

Even over the long-distance connection, Sophie heard the pride in her cousin's voice. "Oh, Mandy, that's really wonderful."

"Yes, I know. I'm so excited. But I'm also so sorry. Poor Joy. She must be terribly upset."

"She is." And she'll be even more upset now.

But Sophie knew none of this was Mandy's fault, so she made sure she sounded as upbeat as possible when she answered, "But I don't want you to worry about it. This isn't your problem. And you have a tremendous opportunity ahead of you." Sophie couldn't help feeling a bit envious. She'd always wanted to travel, had in fact made a start the summer before Joy had come to live with her by spending two weeks in Spain. Since then, though, she'd put her travel plans on hold until Joy went off to college.

"Thanks," Mandy said. The happiness in her voice was unmistakable. "I—I have something else to tell you, too."

"Oh?"

"I've met someone."

Sophie couldn't help smiling. "That's wonderful. Who is he?"

"He's someone new here. He manages the

IT department. His name is Jake Fleming." She paused for a moment. "Oh, Sophie, he's wonderful."

"How's that going to work…with you in Europe…and him in LA?"

"I don't know, but he wants it to work as much as I do, so we'll figure something out. We can always do long weekends."

Mandy sounded so happy that Sophie didn't want to throw cold water on her optimistic plans. But long-distance relationships were tough to maintain. Still, if Mandy and her new man wanted it badly enough, they'd work it out.

The two cousins talked awhile longer; then Sophie regretfully said goodbye.

"She said no, didn't she?" Joy said when Sophie rejoined her in the living room where Joy was eating Cheetos, watching a rerun of

Modern Family and halfheartedly doing her Spanish homework.

Sophie nodded and explained what Mandy had told her.

"What am I going to do now?" Joy said.

"I don't know." Sophie had been frantically trying to think of someone else, somewhere else Joy could go. But there was nowhere else. Mandy's mother—Joy and Sophie's aunt Laureen—lived in Tucson, but she suffered from a form of Parkinson's and lived in a fifty-five-and-over assisted-living community. She couldn't possibly take Joy. And Joy's only other relative was her father's younger brother, but he was single and worked for an oil company and traveled all over the world.

"I don't want to go live in some kind of *home*," Joy said.

"I wouldn't send you anywhere like that."

"Then what're we gonna do?"

Sophie sighed. "Honestly? I don't know."

"Maybe I should just stay here."

"It would be hard."

"I know."

"Think you could do it?"

Joy shrugged. "Other girls have done it. Kara Lee Tompkins did it."

Sophie remembered how hard it had been for Kara Lee and especially for Kara Lee's parents, because her father was the minister at the First Baptist Church here in Crandall Lake and Kara Lee herself had been the director of the children's choir there. Lots of not-so-nice-things had been said about the teenager, especially when it was realized the father of the girl's baby was the son of the church custodian and Hispanic. Crandall Lake wasn't exactly a liberal-thinking town.

"How *is* Kara Lee?" Sophie asked. "Do you know?"

"She's at Baylor now," Joy said. "Last I heard, she was doing great."

"And she gave her baby up for adoption, didn't she?"

Joy looked thoughtful. "I think one of her dad's brothers took the baby. Their family lives in Houston."

Sophie nodded. Although she'd always loved Crandall Lake, at that moment she wished they lived in a big city, too. Big cities were much more forgiving. If only she had the kind of job where she could move easily, she'd give her notice, pack up and take Joy to Houston or Dallas and never look back. After all, what would she actually be leaving?

Dillon.

You'd be leaving Dillon.

She'd also be leaving the job she loved, the job she'd only won two years ago. Did she *really* want to do that? How would it look to other school districts if she left Crandall Lake High School in the lurch? Would anyone else even want to hire her under those circumstances? "You know what? We don't have to decide anything today. Let me think about this for a day or two. Then we'll talk again."

"Okay," Joy said.

But even as Sophie headed toward the kitchen to start preparations for their dinner, she knew that all the thinking in the world wasn't going to give her some magic solution. And from the expression on Joy's face when she'd left her, Sophie knew Joy realized that, too.

Chapter Six

Sophie hadn't intended to tell Beth about Joy, but that weekend, after two more days of agonizing over the problem, she gave in to the temptation to confide in her best friend.

"Oh, Sophie, I'm so sorry," Beth said. Her brown eyes were warm with sympathy.

"Thank you."

"Have you looked into any of those places that take girls in this predicament?"

"Actually, I have, even though I know Joy would be horrified if she knew."

"And?"

"And it's not like it used to be years ago. There are some wonderful places where Joy could go and be with other girls like her. Places where she could live, go to school, take some college-level art courses, and then have her baby." Sophie tried to make her voice upbeat, but it was hard because bottom line, Sophie didn't *want* Joy to go away. She would miss her.

"So what are you going to do?"

"I don't know. I wish…"

"What?"

Sophie sighed deeply, giving voice for the first time to what she *really* wanted to do. "I know this will sound crazy, but I…I wish she could just stay here, have her baby, and…let me raise it for her."

Beth's mouth dropped open. "You're kidding." When Sophie only stared at her, she said, "You're not kidding."

"No."

"I never knew you *wanted* a baby."

"I've *always* wanted a baby. I just didn't talk about it." For days now, Joy's coming baby had been like a magnet in Sophie's mind. She'd been unable to leave the thought alone for more than minutes. She almost felt the way she knew her mother would have felt over a first grandchild.

"If you feel that way, why not talk to Joy about it? Maybe she'd be happy to do just that."

"I don't know. She's embarrassed and worried about what all the kids will say."

"That would blow over."

"Maybe." But Sophie wasn't sure. "Thing is, if...well, if it were some other boy..."

Beth nodded. "Yeah. I was thinking that,

but I didn't want to say it. The fact that he's Dillon's nephew complicates things. It's also kind of ironic, don't you think?"

"Why? Because once upon a time Dillon and I were an item? That's an old story, Beth."

"Is it?" Beth's eyes seemed to see right through her.

Sophie could feel her face heating.

"I knew it!" Beth said. "You've been seeing Dillon again."

"It's not like that..." Sophie began. "It's just that I've had to talk to him about Joy."

"Oh, really?" Beth looked skeptical. "And that's all?"

But even as Sophie started to say *of course that's all*, she couldn't meet Beth's eyes. She sighed, then shrugged. "I'm not going to see him again." When Beth gave her a look of disbelief, Sophie added defensively, "Nothing has changed, Beth. He's still the same love-

’em-and-leave-’em Dillon Burke. And I have no intention of being left again.”

“How far has this gone?”

“We’ve just talked, that’s all.”

“Really? And I suppose you don’t feel anything for Dillon.”

“No, I don’t.”

“Sophie, you’re not a good liar.” When Sophie didn’t answer, Beth reached across the table and squeezed her hand. “Just be careful, Sophie, will you? I don’t want to see you getting hurt again.”

Beth’s words haunted Sophie for the rest of the day. Beth was right. She *wasn’t* a good liar. And, unfortunately for her, she *did* care about Dillon. She cared way too much.

Darn it! She had to stop thinking about him and concentrate all her energy on a solution to the immediate problem of Joy and her baby instead.

* * *

"You've been avoiding me." Dillon knew he was right when Sophie didn't meet his eyes. "Why? Don't you think we need to talk?"

"Yes, I do, but honestly, Dillon, I didn't know what I was going to say when we did."

"I realize this is a complicated situation, but it's not going to change by us ignoring it. I think, for everyone's sake, we need to come to a decision."

She bit her lip. "You're right." Looking around nervously—they were standing in the middle of the hallway outside the office—she added in a lower voice, "But we can't talk here."

"I know that. So why don't we go and get a bite to eat somewhere tonight? We can talk then."

"I don't think it's a good idea for us to—"

He frowned. "For us to what?"

"You know. Be seen together outside of school."

"Oh, for crying out loud, Sophie. What's wrong with us being seen together outside of school? We're both free and we're not kids."

"Well, I just thought—"

"What'd you just think?" Dillon was trying not to get mad, but what was wrong with her? You'd think he had some contagious disease or something the way she'd been avoiding him.

She blew out a breath. "I just wanted to avoid gossip." She shifted to her other leg and repositioned the books she was carrying. The action caused her red T-shirt to tighten across her breasts.

Dillon hated the way his body immediately reacted to her, no matter what she did. What the hell was it about this woman that affected him so strongly? You'd think he'd never been around a sexy woman before. "There's gonna be a heckuva lot of gossip that'll be way worse than seeing the two of us together before all this is over," he muttered.

"Not if we play things right."

Something about the way she said that told Dillon she was hiding something, because there wasn't any conviction in her voice. Just then the bell signaling the start of the sixth period sounded, and she jumped.

Dillon needed to get out on the football field, where the team was waiting for him. "I'll pick you up at six-thirty. We can talk more then."

She looked as if she wanted to argue with him, but after a moment, she just nodded. "Okay."

As Dillon walked toward the stadium, he decided that he was tired of Sophie calling all the shots. From now on, he was going to take charge. And if she didn't like it, too bad.

He grinned. A good offense was always better than a good defense.

He sure was high-handed.

Sophie guessed Dillon thought he'd scored some points or something. Well, she'd straighten him out tonight. But before that, she needed to talk to Joy. See what she thought about Sophie's idea. Maybe she'd be in favor of it. Sophie tried not to get her hopes up, but now that she'd admitted how much she'd like to raise Joy's baby, maybe even *adopt* the baby, she could hardly think about anything else. It was if the mother gene had been awakened in her, and now that it had, it wasn't going to go away.

During sixth period, which was a time Sophie could spend catching up on paperwork or counseling students or anything else she deemed important, she texted Joy and asked her to come straight home after school.

We need to talk, she said.

K, Joy texted back. C U then.

Joy was already at the house when Sophie arrived. Dropping her books and tote on the nearest chair, Sophie headed straight for the fridge. She was dying for iced tea After pouring herself a glass, she asked Joy if she wanted one.

"No, I'm fine," Joy said. She had abandoned the painting she'd been working on and, following Sophie, had plopped onto one of the kitchen chairs. Reaching for a banana from the bowl of fruit in the middle of the table, she began to peel it. She made a face. "Lately, I'm always hungry."

"You're feeding two."

"Yeah. I know."

Sophie wished the circumstances were different. That the knowledge she was carrying a baby would have put a smile on Joy's face instead of that glum, resigned expression. "Listen, I've had an idea, and I wanted to see what you think."

"Okay."

Sophie took a deep breath. "How would you feel about staying here to have your baby? And once it's born, letting me raise it?"

Joy stared at her. "Staying *here*? Letting *you* raise it?"

"Yes."

"But, Sophie—"

"I know. Everyone will know. But you know what the alternative is. You'll have to go away somewhere where you don't know anyone, where you'll have your baby alone, where you won't be able to see Aidan anymore, where I won't be able to visit you very often." She didn't add, *Where some stranger will take your baby and we won't ever see it again.* "Do you *want* to go away?"

Joy shook her head. "But I was thinking… why can't I go to London?"

"*London?* With Mandy, you mean?"

"Yes."

"Mandy didn't offer, and I won't ask her. Anyway, it's a terrible idea."

"Why is it a terrible idea?"

"Because of health insurance, for one thing. And for another, Mandy is going to be extremely busy with a responsible new position. She won't have time to take care of you. And she shouldn't have to. You're not her responsibility. You're mine. No. Going out of the country is not an option."

Joy slumped ever farther down in her chair. "I don't want everyone to know. I—I can't face them."

"Then I guess we'll have to pick a place. One of the homes I researched is in San Antonio. Going there would have quite a few advantages."

"Like what?"

"Well, If you went there, it's close enough I could come to see you every other weekend or so."

Joy nodded. But her eyes were bleak.

"Plus, they not only have an art institute but the Southwest School of Art is there—it's got a terrific reputation—and you would be able to take some classes. I looked at their curriculum and they offer jewelry and metals, printmaking and mixed media, digital media and a whole lot of other classes through their Community Education Program." The courses Sophie had mentioned weren't available anywhere near Crandall Lake and were all areas Joy had expressed an interest in.

Joy still looked as if she wanted to cry.

Sophie felt sorry for her, but if her sister wouldn't consider staying in Crandall Lake, then this would be the best solution. "Even if you go away, I'd still like you to think about me adopting the baby."

"You'd *really* want to do that?"

"Yes, I would."

"I thought you were just saying that because you thought it's what I'd like to hear."

"No, it's what I really want."

"And the baby wouldn't know I was its real mother?"

"Not if you didn't want him to know."

Joy didn't answer for a long moment. Then she shrugged. "I guess it would be okay."

"You don't sound sure."

Another shrug. "It…it would be hard. But if you want to…"

"I do want to, but I want you to want it, too.

I won't do it if it bothers you or you feel you can't live with it. I realize it would be easier for you if the baby went to someone else."

"Can I think about that part for a while?"

"Yes. But, Joy…"

"Yes?"

"You might not think so now, but years from now, I think it would make you feel good to know who your baby is and where he is and to be able to see him and be a part of his life even if he never does know you're his birth mother."

Joy didn't answer, but her eyes were thoughtful, and Sophie knew she would really think about what Sophie had said. Now all Sophie could do was hope she'd come to the same conclusion.

I want that baby.

That might be selfish on Sophie's part, but she couldn't help how she felt. "I'm going out to dinner with Dillon tonight. We're going to talk about your decision. So I'll make you something before I go, okay?"

"Can I just order a pizza? And can Aidan come over? I want to talk about this with him, too."

"Of course."

Sophie left Joy still sitting in the kitchen when she went upstairs to shower and change.

The grandfather clock in the foyer had just begun to chime the half hour when the doorbell rang.

"Right on time," Sophie said when she opened the door. She'd changed into a black pencil skirt, black ballerina flats and a pale aqua sweater. And she'd tamed her unruly hair with a matching aqua silk ribbon. She saw that Dillon, too, had changed. Tonight he wore pressed khaki pants and a dark blue shirt. She wondered if he'd picked the color to match his eyes. The thought made her grin.

"What're you smiling about?" he said.

"Just wondering if you picked that shirt to match your eyes."

He gave her a mock scowl. "Men don't think about things like that."

"Really?"

Before he could answer, Joy came out of the dining room where she'd been doing her homework. "Hi," she said.

"Hello, Joy. Aidan said to tell you he'd be here in a few minutes."

"Thanks."

"You ready?" Dillon said to Sophie.

"Yes." Turning to Joy, Sophie said, "We won't be late."

A few minutes later, Sophie was seated next to Dillon in his truck. "Where are we going?"

"I thought Genaro's. Unless you'd prefer somewhere else?"

"I, uh, no, Genaro's is fine." But Sophie wasn't sure if she really wanted to go to the popular Italian eatery. Yet she didn't want to admit this to Dillon, because she was afraid he'd guess why. Thing was, at one time, Genaro's had been their favorite restaurant. She wondered if Dillon had remembered, too.

When they pulled into Genaro's parking lot, Sophie saw that there were already quite a few diners there. "Um, maybe this isn't such a good idea."

"Why not?"

"It's already kind of crowded, don't you think?"

"Doesn't matter. I called Joe. He said he'd save a table for us."

"That wasn't what I was thinking about."

"What *were* you thinking about?"

"Well, an awful lot of people will see us together."

"So?"

"So do we really want a lot of gossip about us?"

Dillon sighed heavily. "You know, Sophie, you act like there's something wrong with us going out together. I told you before. We're both free, we're both single, why *shouldn't* we be out for dinner?"

Sophie wanted to say, *Because I don't want the other women at school to be saying things to me about you, because I don't want them to think we have some kind of relationship going on, because you broke my heart once and I'm afraid you're going to do it again!*

But of course she said none of these things. "You're right. I'm sorry. Let's go inside."

Ten minutes later, settled at a corner table that afforded them a bit of privacy, Joe himself, the owner of Genaro's, poured each of them a glass of the house Chianti, told them their salads and bread would be there soon and walked away smiling.

Several of the other diners had greeted them: the parents of the wide receiver on Dillon's team, the principal of the Catholic Elementary School and her husband and two women Sophie knew from the water aerobics class she'd taken over the summer.

Sophie relaxed a bit as they drank their wine. She was grateful none of the other teachers from the high school were there tonight. Maybe she'd dodged a bullet. But just as the thought crossed her mind, who should walk in but Nicole Blanchard and a tall man Sophie didn't know? Sophie tried to shrink down in her seat, but it was too late. Nicole saw her, and after her first shocked look, she headed straight over to their table, the tall man following her.

"Well, look who's here. Hello, Sophie. Hello, Dillon." Nicole smiled sweetly, but her eyes shot daggers at Sophie.

"Hello, Nicole," Sophie and Dillon said at the same time. They both smiled. Sophie looked pointedly at Nicole's date. "Hi," she said to him.

"Hi." He looked uncomfortable.

"I don't believe we've met," Dillon said, standing politely.

"Oh," Nicole said. "This is Alan. Alan, this is Dillon Burke. You know, the new coach at the high school. He used to play for the Los Angeles Lions." She ignored Sophie.

Sophie bit back a grin. Same old Nicole.

"I knew it was you," no-last-name Alan said. "I've been a fan for years. Best thing the high school's done in a long time, hiring you."

"Well, thanks," Dillon said. He turned to Sophie. "This is Sophie Marlowe. She's the counselor at the high school."

After a few more seconds of inconsequential chitchat, Nicole's date finally managed to pry her away and they were seated across the room.

"Oh, brother," Sophie said as they both sat down again.

"Yeah, she's a pain."

Sophie could just imagine what Nicole would have to say the following day, but there was nothing to be done about it. Just then, their waiter brought their salads and a basket of hot bread, so for the next few minutes they ate without talking. Once the salads were gone, though, Dillon said, "So, did you and Joy decide anything?"

"I think so. I suggested she might like to just stay here to have her baby, but she doesn't want to. I think she and I will go to San Antonio this weekend and visit this home I found. Online it looks great, but I want to see it in person and let Joy meet the people there before making a decision."

"What's the place like?"

Sophie described what she'd read and seen in photos. "It looks really nice. Plus, Joy could take some evening classes at the Southwest School of Art."

"That should soften the blow a little," Dillon said.

"Yes." Sophie debated if and when she should tell him the rest. For some reason, she felt reluctant to do so.

"You seem hesitant," Dillon said, pouring more wine in each of their glasses.

"Not about the home. I…" She drank some of her wine to give her a few minutes.

"If not about the place, then what?"

"I want to adopt Joy's baby."

There. She'd said it. She met Dillon's eyes defiantly.

He looked completely taken aback.

"Well? Say something."

He seemed stunned. "I don't know *what* to say."

"Why are you so shocked?"

"I guess because I had no idea you felt this way."

"I didn't know I felt this way, either," Sophie admitted. "But I do." She met his gaze. "It's a good idea, don't you think?"

"You're the only one who can answer that, Sophie."

Before she could make a rejoinder, their waiter approached with their food: mushroom ravioli for Sophie and the house special lasagna for Dillon. Sophie waited till the waiter had departed before saying, "This is something I really want, Dillon."

"A baby," he said.

"*This* baby," she said.

He nodded, then took a bite of his lasagna. "Okay," he finally answered. "Then, yes, I think it's a good idea. For *you.* But what about Joy? What about Aidan?"

"What about them?" She speared a piece of her ravioli.

"Maybe it's not such a good idea for them."

"Why do you say that?"

"Don't you think it'll just keep reminding them of what they did that they shouldn't have done? Don't you think it might be hard for them?"

"Possibly. But I think it might be harder to just give away their baby to some stranger. To not ever see that baby again. When they're both older, they might really regret having done that."

Dillon nodded. He put down his fork and leaned toward her earnestly. "What if...just what if...one day one or both of them decide they want their baby? What will you do then?"

Sophie stared at him. "It will be a legal adoption, Dillon. I wouldn't settle for anything less." But could she really stick to that decision? Would she be able to deny Joy her child if Joy should sometime decide she wanted that child?

Did Sophie really want to open this can of worms?

Chapter Seven

"And your sister wants to *adopt* the baby?"

Joy nodded. She and Aidan were sitting close together on the couch in the living room. They hadn't turned on any lights, so the only light came from the lamp on the table in the foyer. "What do you think?"

"I don't know. It…it won't really affect me," Aidan said. "'Cause I won't be coming back here after college."

Joy's heart constricted. She'd known he felt this way. She'd figured she'd never see him again once he left Crandall Lake. But suspecting and hearing him put it into words were two different things. She guessed down deep she'd always hoped they'd stay in touch, and that maybe someday they'd get together again. But he obviously didn't feel that way.

"How do *you* feel about it?" Aidan said. "You're the one who's going to have to live with it."

"I don't know what to think. But Sophie wants it..." And in some ways, it *would* be good to know where her baby was and how he was doing. Besides, now that she knew how Aidan felt, Joy figured she probably wouldn't be coming back to Crandall Lake, either, once she started at a college or art school, except for summer vacations. So it wouldn't be as if she'd have to see their child every day. And as she got older and had her own career and family, she wouldn't see much of him at all.

"It'll make her happy," she finished in a rush, trying not to think that Aidan would not be a part of her future at all. That she wouldn't see *anything* of him. That every time she *did* see their child, there would be this ache in her heart. *I'll never be able to forget Aidan if Sophie is raising our baby.*

"Then, fine. Let her do it."

Joy tried to swallow against the lump in her throat. "Will...you come to see me in San Antonio?"

"I don't know, Joy. If...you aren't gonna be here, then maybe Dillon'll let me go back to Ohio for the rest of the school year."

Now Joy's heart thumped painfully, and she was afraid she might burst into tears. "You... you're thinking of going *away*? *Now?* Before I even *have* the baby?"

"*You'll* be going away," he pointed out.

"But Aidan...I thought...I thought we'd be at least be together through this. I thought you'd *want* to be with me. This is your baby, too!" She couldn't control the tears anymore, and they dripped down her face.

Aidan hung his head. "I'm sorry. I—I..."

He couldn't even look at her. Joy ignored the pain in her chest and angrily brushed the tears away. Jumping up, she glared at him. "I—I thought you were different, Aidan. I thought you really cared about me. But you don't, do you? I was just somebody convenient to make you feel better because you were lonely. You never thought about me at all, did you? Okay. Fine. Go away. I really don't care. In fact, I don't care if I ever see you again."

"Joy..." He reached for her. "I *do* care about you. I just—"

"No!" she said, jumping back and slapping his hands away. "Go home. Just go home."

Now he stood, and this time he tried to gather her into his arms.

"Don't touch me!" Joy moved out of his grasp. "I mean it, Aidan. Go home. And don't…don't call me or text me or try to talk to me at school. We're finished!"

And with that, she walked out of the room and into the dining room, where her paintings had always comforted her. She closed the door after her. Even then, even after what she'd said, she thought he'd come after her. That he'd say he was sorry, that he hadn't meant any of it, that he was just upset, but that he loved her and wanted to be with her while she carried their baby.

It was only when she heard the front door open and close that she sank down onto the floor and cried her eyes out.

"Where are you going?" Sophie said. Dillon wasn't headed toward her house. The truck was pointed in the opposite direction.

"It's a nice night. Full moon. I thought I'd drive out to the lake."

"The lake?" Sophie said weakly. God, that was all she needed. To go out to Crandall Lake, the scene where they'd made out too many times to count. "That's not a good idea, Dillon. The kids still go out there all the time. Someone will see us."

"I'll drive around to the north side. I just want to sit and look at the lake in the moon-light. With you." His voice had softened and he reached over to take her hand.

Sophie pulled it away. Her heart was already going double time, just at the *thought* of being out at the lake with Dillon. "This is a bad idea. You need to take me home."

"Oh, c'mon, Sophie. Don't be like that. I won't do anything you don't want me to do. I promise."

That's what she was afraid of. Trouble was,

she wanted him to do every single thing they'd ever done together. And even though she knew that would be another mistake to add to the one she'd already made, she also knew she had no willpower where he was concerned. "Please, Dillon. Take me home. Okay?"

But he ignored her, turning on the radio instead. When something soft and beautiful, an instrumental love song, began to play, she realized he had Sirius. She sighed. She knew when she was beaten.

Ten minutes later, he pulled down a private driveway leading to the north side of the lake—the side lined with large, beautiful homes. "I don't think you're allowed to drive on this road," she said.

"Who's going to see us?" So saying, he turned off the headlights.

A few minutes later, with only the moon-light to guide them, he stopped. The lake was only about six feet ahead of them. He lowered the windows, allowing the cool night air in. The water shimmered and lapped gently, and somewhere in the distance, an owl hooted.

Slipping his arm around her, he pulled her closer. Sophie didn't even try to resist. What was the point?

And when he whispered "Sophie..." and lowered his head to capture her mouth in a kiss, she closed her eyes and gave herself up to him.

She'd forgotten how difficult it could be to make love in a car. Difficult but incredibly exciting because no matter how private the area might seem, no matter how they might feel protected and enclosed by the night, there was an inescapable element of danger. That element lent an edge to the desire flooding her, and Sophie knew she wasn't going to say no. In fact, she wasn't going to deny him anything. She was his for the taking.

She gasped as the cool air hit her naked skin, sucked in her breath as his mouth covered her breasts. When, just before entering her, he put on a condom, she knew he'd been thinking about this even before he picked her up tonight. But then, if she was being truthful, she'd been thinking about it, too. "Sophie!" he cried as they shuddered together in a climax that came so fast and so hard it made Sophie's heart feel as if it were going to pound right out of her chest.

"I haven't been able to think about anything else since the other night," he muttered once they'd both quieted and were lying twined together.

"I noticed you came prepared," she said drily.

"Hey, I was a Boy Scout."

She couldn't help laughing, even though she knew later tonight, once she was alone, she would probably regret everything she'd allowed him to do and every single thing she'd said.

"I've missed you, Sophie," he said later while nuzzling her ear.

She shivered, whispering back, "I've missed you, too."

"We were always good together."

"Yes." She sighed deeply. "Dillon?"

"Yeah?"

"My back hurts. It's awfully cramped in this car."

"Oh, I'm sorry." He pushed himself up, then helped her sit up.

For the next few minutes, they managed to retrieve their clothes and get dressed again.

"I think we'd better get home," she said, not looking at him. Now that she was once again fully clothed, she felt embarrassed. What was wrong with her that she had absolutely no backbone or resistance where he was concerned?

They didn't talk much on the way to her house. And when they got there, she hurriedly opened the door on her side and hopped out. But he was faster than she was and before she'd taken more than a few steps up the walk, he was there with her.

"What are you doing, Sophie?" he asked, taking her arm so she couldn't escape. "Are you mad at me?"

"No, Dillon, I'm not mad at you." But there was an ache somewhere in the vicinity of her heart.

"Then why are you trying to run away from me? I—I care about you, Sophie. I want to see you again."

You want sex again. Why don't you just say what you mean? "I'll have to think about that."

"I don't understand you. You admitted you missed me. You agreed that we're good together. And now you have to *think* about it?"

He was still holding on to her arm, so she couldn't get away without making a federal case out of the attempt. "It's complicated. You know that, Dillon."

"I don't see how. You like me, I like you, we're damn good together and neither one of us is in a relationship with anyone else. Why is it complicated?"

Sophie sighed. "Well, for one thing, there's the little matter of Joy and Aidan and their baby. For another, I'm not sure I'm in a good place to be making decisions right now." *And most important, all I've heard is the word* like, *which is a lukewarm word at best.*

"Sophie…"

"Dillon."

"Don't do this."

"I'm sorry. But I really do need some time."

"You're punishing me, aren't you?"

Oh God. He's not going to let it go. "I'm not punishing you. I'm just trying to be sensible."

"You're punishing me because I went off to college and left you. But, Sophie, I never promised you I'd stay."

"Dillon, I'm not going to have this conversation tonight. It's late, and I'm really tired and I want to go inside, see how Joy is doing and then go to bed." So saying, she finally pulled free of his grasp. "Thanks for dinner. And good night."

And this time she didn't wait for him to say anything. She simply walked to the door, opened it and closed it behind her.

Dammit, anyway.

He knew what she'd wanted him to say. She'd wanted him to say he loved her, that he couldn't live without her and that he wanted her to marry him.

But he couldn't say that. Not unless he meant it. And he didn't know if he did. Yes, he cared about her. And yes, he thought about her all the time. And yes, he wanted her.

But love? Marriage?

Dillon wasn't sure he was cut out for the marriage thing. Not to mention the fact Sophie intended to keep and raise Joy's baby. She'd be a package deal.

So he damn sure wasn't going to say anything he wasn't certain he wholeheartedly meant, nor was he going to make her any promises he wasn't certain he could keep.

He hit the steering wheel in frustration.

Damn!

Joy's bedroom door was closed when Sophie went upstairs. She paused outside it, wondering if Joy was asleep or simply didn't want to see or talk to Sophie again today. Deciding that a closed door sent a message, and that she was too tired to talk to Joy again anyway, Sophie headed for her own bedroom.

Later, teeth brushed, face moisturized, she was tucked into bed and allowed herself to finally think about Dillon.

"I care about you. We're good together. I want to see you again."

Noticeably absent were the only three words Sophie really cared about. *I love you.* She whispered them to herself. Would she ever hear them from Dillon? Or was she kidding herself yet again?

She knew Dillon was gun-shy.

She also knew he was afraid of commitment.

Oh, he didn't have to say so. His past actions had said it all.

Face it, Sophie. You are letting yourself in for big-time heartbreak this time. Last time, you were just a kid. At sixteen and seventeen, heartbreak is part of the lexicon. But you're not a kid anymore. And the kind of heartbreak Dillon can deliver will make the old heart-break seem like a walk in the park.

You're going to be seriously hurt in this fool's game you're playing. So you know what you need to do. You need to get out now. Before it's too late. Before he takes that heart of yours and smashes it into a million pieces where all the king's horses and all the king's men won't be able to put it together again.

The next day, when Sophie walked into the teachers' lounge to eat her lunch, she cringed at the sight of Nicole Blanchard. *Oh God,* she thought, *I'm in for it.* She knew, just by the expression Nicole's face, that the subject of

Sophie's dinner with Dillon last night was going to be the next topic of conversation. Maybe she could pretend she'd forgotten to do something and leave.

"Well, well, well," Nicole said. "And here she is. We were just talking about you, Sophie."

Sophie sighed inwardly. So much for making a fast exit. "Hi, guys." She smiled at the other teachers sitting with Nicole—Cindy Bloom and Jackie Farrow. Deciding she would not give Nicole the satisfaction of asking what they'd been saying about her, she calmly opened her lunch bag and took out her tuna sandwich.

"You sure are a sly one," Nicole said archly.

"Oh?" Sophie said. She took a bite of her sandwich. She had no intention of giving Nicole an inch more than she had to.

"You never mentioned that you were dating Dillon."

"That's because I'm not." God would forgive her for telling a lie.

Nicole made a disbelieving sound. "Having dinner with him at Genaro's? You don't call *that* a date?"

"I call it dinner with an old friend."

"An old *friend*?"

"Sophie knows Dillon from high school," put in Jackie, who had also been a cheerleader during Sophie's tenure.

Nicole frowned. "So you're *not* dating him?"

"That's what I said." Sophie continued to eat her sandwich, but she could have hugged Jackie for sounding so matter-of-fact and doing Sophie's work for her.

Nicole smiled. "So the field's still wide-open."

"As far as I know," Sophie said. She almost felt sorry for Dillon as she saw the wheels turning in Nicole's head, but then she decided he deserved whatever was coming his way.

And he would certainly be able to handle it.

She was just glad to have deflected Nicole's curiosity, because even worse than being dumped by Dillon a second time would be having everyone in Crandall Lake know it.

Especially little Miss Nicole.

Over the weekend, Joy and Sophie drove to San Antonio and visited Hannah's House, the home for expectant mothers that Sophie had researched and decided was the best of all the options available. It turned out to be everything she'd imagined and more. The facility was set in a green and tranquil area near downtown and the river, but secluded behind hundreds of trees and a high brick wall that made it feel like a serene oasis. It had been founded by the Episcopal church and was staffed partly by nuns and partly by trained staff, including half a dozen experienced midwives and nurses. It was beautiful, and each guest/expectant mother had the choice of sharing a room with one other roommate or having a private room.

All the young women there seemed friendly, and when Sophie and Joy were having their tour, they were approached several times by welcoming occupants. By the time they finished their tour, Sophie was sold, and so was Joy. In fact, she smiled for the first time that day when she told Sophie she'd like to come there.

The cost was high, but Sophie had already known it would be. As per their agreement, she texted Dillon to tell him they both loved the place and she wanted to sign Joy up. She quoted the cost and waited for his reply, which arrived in minutes.

No problem on my end. If you're okay with it, sign her up.

Sophie felt as if a tremendous weight had been lifted from her shoulders. She and Joy filled out the paperwork, and both signed permission forms for various things, including medical care, schooling, supervision and adherence to the rules. Sophie wrote a check for the down payment on a private room, and Joy was given a list of what she needed to bring and what she wasn't allowed to bring.

They both shook hands with Sister Monica, and Sophie said they would be back on Wednesday, as long as she could take the day off. "If not, then it'll have to be next Saturday."

Sophie had made a reservation for them at the Marriott on the River Walk, and she was determined she and Joy would enjoy this day away from Crandall Lake. They shopped,

Sophie buying Joy some cute clothes that would work as she grew bigger, and then Joy encouraged Sophie to buy herself something. Seeing a gorgeous rust-colored wool skirt paired with a pale yellow silk blouse that was perfect for Sophie's coloring, she decided to splurge and get herself an early Christmas present.

Later they had dinner at one of the riverside restaurants and Sophie allowed herself a couple of glasses of wine. "I'm not driving," she said with a smile at Joy, who actually seemed happy today.

"I think I'll like it here," Joy said, taking a drink of her iced tea. "I'm excited about signing up for one of the art courses." In the morning they planned to visit the art institute as well as the art college.

"You'll still have to take all the required

courses—Spanish and geometry, American history."

"I know."

"And it won't be easy with new teachers."

"I know, Sophie. Don't worry."

But Sophie knew she *would* worry. Sure, she had been reassuring Joy and telling her everything would be fine, but she was realistic enough to know that Joy was going to have some tough days. Days when she would be homesick and lonely. Days when her pregnancy would bother her. Days when she would want nothing more than to turn the clock back.

"What did Aidan have to say about all this?" Sophie finally asked. She'd avoided the question because Joy hadn't seemed to want to discuss it before, but the time felt right now.

"Aidan doesn't want to be involved in this. And I don't want him to be, either," Joy said tightly, her eyes darkening.

“He said that?”

“He said he hoped he could persuade his uncle to let him go back to Ohio to finish out his senior year and after that he has no intention of ever coming back to Texas again.”

Sophie understood Joy was trying to act as if she didn’t care, but underneath the facade of nonchalance, Sophie saw the hurt and desolation. Sophie’s heart ached for Joy. The poor kid. Bad enough to find herself in this tough spot, but horrible to find out the boy she thought she loved had feet of clay.

“Kaitlyn warned me,” Joy added bitterly, “when I talked to her that time, but I told her she was wrong. Just because Billy Newhouse deserted *her* the moment he found out she was pregnant, Aidan wasn’t going to do that to me. Not Aidan. Ha!” Tears shone in her eyes.

“Honey…” Sophie leaned across the table

and put her hand over Joy's. "He's awfully young."

"Not too young to get me pregnant!"

"I know. But still…"

"Oh, don't make excuses for him, Sophie. He couldn't wait to get away from me. He wants no part of this."

Sophie sighed, releasing Joy's hand. "Well, we don't need him. You didn't want to marry him, anyway. Both of you agreed you're too young to be parents. So maybe this is best. A clean, fast break."

Joy nodded, but she still looked crestfallen.

"It could be worse. He could have deserted you without any financial support, either." Billy Newhouse had tried just that, insisting Kaitlyn Lowe, the senior Sophie had counseled earlier in the year, have a DNA test. His ploy hadn't worked because he *was* the father of Kaitlyn's baby. So even though he wanted no part of her pregnancy, he was still going to be liable financially.

"Yeah, I know," Joy said.

"So, c'mon. Cheer up. Hannah's House is a wonderful place, and I think you're going to be happy there."

It took a few seconds, but finally Joy smiled again. "Thank you, Sophie. I love you."

"I know, honey. I love you, too."

Dillon wasn't surprised when Aidan said he wanted to go back to Ohio to finish out his senior year. And even though Dillon had been against the idea earlier in the year, now he thought it might be best for everyone. Certainly Sophie would be happy to see the kid's backside. So Dillon made a couple of phone calls, and later on Sunday afternoon he cornered Aidan in the living room, where his nephew was sprawled on the couch watching Ohio State play.

"I talked to Scooter Davis this morning." Scooter was an old friend of Dillon's from his college days. More important, Scooter was on the baseball coaching staff at Ohio State.

Aidan looked up.

"He's agreed to keep an eye on you, kind of be your de facto guardian for the rest of the school year. He said there are a couple of empty condos in the building where he lives and he'd check into rentals for me."

"You're gonna let me go?" Aidan's voice squeaked in his excitement.

"You didn't think I would?"

Aidan shook his head. His eyes were alight with an excitement Dillon hadn't seen in a long time.

"There are lots of details to work out, not the least of which is the kind of behavior I expect from you. There are going to be a lot of rules, Aidan. You are not going to do anything you want just because I'm not there."

"I know, I know. And I promise you, I'll follow all the rules. All of them." Aidan's voice actually shook.

The kid looked so happy and hopeful Dillon didn't know whether to laugh or cry. All he really knew was that Aidan couldn't wait to get away from Crandall Lake. And him.

"Scooter's going to call me in a couple of days. Just as soon as he has all the information. Until then, we'll just wait and see, okay?"

"Okay."

Dillon turned to walk away but stopped when Aidan said, "Uh, Dillon?"

"Yes?" He turned around.

"Thanks. I—really appreciate this. I know you didn't have to do anything to help me."

Dillon nodded. "You're welcome." But his

heart was heavy as he left the room. It was a damn shame that the first time Aidan had acted happy to have Dillon as his uncle was the day he knew he was going to escape from him.

Chapter Eight

Sophie had no problem getting Wednesday off—she'd talked to Connie Woodson, the assistant principal, who had kindly provided Hannah's House with Sophie's transcript and who was not a gossip and would keep that information to herself. So at ten o'clock, car packed with Joy's things, the two sisters set off again for San Antonio. It was a two-and-a-half-hour drive and they stopped for lunch along the way, so it was a little after two before they arrived. Sophie had texted ahead to say when they would be there, so Sister Monica's assistant, a pretty young woman named Michelle, greeted them.

"Your room is all ready," she told Joy. "And the welcoming committee is waiting for you in the common room."

"The welcoming committee?" Joy said.

"We always have a little party for a new resident. After you put your things in your room, come and join us."

When Sophie and Joy entered the common room, Sophie was astonished to see balloons, a cake and ice cream and a small pile of wrapped gifts. Joy seemed stunned.

The other girls beamed as she opened the presents. There were a couple of onesies, several receiving blankets, a pair of crocheted booties with a matching sweater and cap, and a copy of *What to Expect When You're Expecting.*

"This is so sweet," Sophie said to Michelle.

"The girls love doing it."

Sophie could feel tears threatening. These people were so nice. Joy would be happy here. And she would have a happy baby because of it.

My baby, Sophie thought, looking at the gifts. *I'll be using these things.* Somehow the sight of the tiny baby clothes made the baby's coming arrival seem more real.

Sophie stayed another hour, then said her goodbyes. Joy walked her out to her car.

"I'm going to miss you," Sophie said as they hugged.

Joy's eyes glistened with tears. "I'll miss you, too."

"But I think you'll like it here."

Joy nodded. "All the girls seem really nice."

"You can call or text anytime. You know that. And I'll come down as often as I can."

"I know," Joy whispered, hugging Sophie again.

"It's going to be okay."

"I know," Joy said again.

As Sophie drove off, she could see Joy standing in the drive. She looked so small and young. Sophie swallowed against the lump in her throat. Hannah's House was a perfect solution for Joy, and there was nothing to be sad about.

But it took Sophie a long time to shake off her melancholy. In fact, she still hadn't completely shaken it by the time she reached the Crandall Lake city limits.

As if he'd been watching for her return, Sophie's cell rang as she pulled into her garage. Caller ID showed it was Dillon.

"Hi," she said, getting out of her car and closing the garage door.

"Are you back?"

"Just pulled in."

"How'd it go?"

"Very well." She told him about the welcoming committee and the gifts. "Joy's going to be happy there."

"Good."

"What about Aidan? Did you talk to your friend again?" By now Sophie was in the house and she dropped her purse and keys on the kitchen table, then sank into a chair to finish the conversation.

"Yeah, and it's all set. He leaves on Tuesday. Early flight out of DFW."

Sophie nodded, even though Dillon couldn't see her. Part of her was glad Aidan would be gone. The other part of her resented everything about him leaving. For him, it would be as if nothing had ever happened. He would be able to forget about Joy, the baby and his responsibility for the whole thing, whereas

Joy… She would never be able to forget. It just made Sophie so mad. Why was it that women always paid the biggest price for mistakes?

Maybe if you let her put the baby up for adoption to someone else, it would be better. But Sophie didn't want to think along those lines, so she shoved the thought away. It *wouldn't* be better. Even if Joy never set eyes on her baby after it was born, she still wouldn't ever forget. A woman could not give birth, then wipe the whole episode out of her mind.

"Want to get a bite to eat tonight?" Dillon asked.

Sophie started to say no, but Dillon interrupted, saying, "C'mon, it's no big deal, just dinner. I thought we could go to Bob's. There are some things I think we need to talk about."

Bob's Steak House was a local legend. Some reviewers came from as far away as Houston and Dallas and without exception gave Bob's four or five stars. Sophie hadn't been there in months. And then it had been with girlfriends. It was tempting to say yes to Dillon. Besides, he was right. They still *did* have some things they needed to discuss.

"How about I'll pick you up at six?"

"Oh, okay. You talked me into it." After all, she reasoned, what harm could come from just having a steak with him?

But later, as they sat across from each other in the dimly lit restaurant and waited for their steaks to arrive, she knew she had once again been lying to herself. Just looking at Dillon was dangerous. And being in close proximity was foolhardy. He gave off an animal magnetism that couldn't be ignored. Even now, during normal conversation, she found it harder to breathe.

"I wanted to tell you that I made arrangements to have money deposited to your checking account on the first of each month," Dillon said.

"Thank you." Sophie knew Joy was lucky that Aidan had at least accepted financial responsibility for her condition, and that he had the resources to back it up. Hannah's House was expensive, and Sophie would not have been able to manage on her own. Not without tapping into Joy's college fund. Thank goodness that wouldn't be necessary.

"Look," Dillon continued, frowning slightly. "I don't want you to think Aidan's running away. He feels bad about Joy."

"Not that bad." The words were out before Sophie could stop them.

"That's not fair. He's just a kid himself."

Sophie sighed. "I know that, and I don't want to fight about this. What's done is done, and we're doing the best we can. Let's talk about something else."

"Want to talk about how nobody's happy with me as a coach?"

"Seriously? I haven't heard anything about that."

Dillon made a face. "You will. Mayor Ferguson is on the warpath."

"Why?" Funny Beth hadn't said anything. She was the mayor's administrative assistant and usually knew everything.

"Because I didn't play his baby boy the last two weeks."

"I thought Jimmy was still recuperating from his shoulder injury."

"Doc Ford says he's okay to play. Trouble is, Devon Washington's better than Jimmy. In fact, he's terrific, and as far as I'm concerned, Devon's won the starting spot."

Just then their waiter appeared with their

steaks, and for the next few minutes, they were busy fixing their baked potatoes and preparing to eat. But finally Sophie said, "I don't envy you getting on the bad side of the mayor. But you know what? I think the parents will stand behind you. Mayor Ferguson hasn't made a whole lot of friends since he took office." Actually, that was an understatement. Ferguson was so high-handed about any number of things that he'd made quite a few enemies.

"We'll see. He says I won't be offered a new contract."

Sophie frowned. "What do you mean, a new contract?"

"I was only signed on for one year."

"What? Why?"

"Because that's the way I wanted it." He cut off a piece of steak. "I wasn't sure coaching high school football was what I wanted to do, so I figured a trial year made sense."

At that moment, when Sophie realized Aidan might not be the only Burke leaving Crandall Lake for good, she knew that no matter what she'd been telling herself, her secret hope had always been that one of these days Dillon would finally realize he loved her. That they belonged together. She hoped her face didn't betray the dismay she felt. "Everyone here loves having you as the coach."

"Not everyone. I understand there were several other guys considered for the job, and it would be natural for them to resent me."

Sophie nodded. She actually knew a couple of the others who'd interviewed. Dismay turned to fear, and even though she was afraid of the answer, she had to ask, "Do you *want* to stay on at Crandall High?"

Dillon didn't say anything for a moment.

When he did, his voice was thoughtful. "I honestly don't know. I'll have to see what they offer me." He paused, looked at her. "How you feel about it will enter into my decision, too."

"How *I* feel about it?" To hide her confusion, she ate some of her baked potato.

"Don't look so surprised. Hell, I don't know what you think, whether you want me around or whether you wish I'd disappear. And once you're raising the kids' baby, it might be better for everyone concerned if I was gone."

Sophie couldn't think what to say. She was so upset by what he'd just said that she was afraid she'd burst into tears if she wasn't careful. Did he really think that was what she wanted? For him to go away? She'd *never* wanted him to go away. *He'd* been the one who couldn't wait to leave. And now he was thinking about doing it again!

"Leaving when the going gets tough seems to be a speciality of the Burke men."

His eyes narrowed, and he put down his fork. "Is that what you think? That I'm looking for a way out?"

"I don't know. Why don't you tell me?"

"That's not what I meant, and you know it."

"I think you made it perfectly clear."

"What is it with you women? You enjoy twisting words, don't you? I *never* said I wanted to leave."

Suddenly Sophie'd had enough. She was tired of him blowing hot and cold. Tired of always being the one left behind. Tired of wanting something that obviously didn't exist. And she no longer cared what anyone might think. She put down her fork, laid her napkin on the table and stood up. Keeping her voice low so the other diners wouldn't hear her, she said, "You know, Dillon, as far as I'm concerned, you can leave town anytime you want, and good riddance, to you *and* your nephew. Now, just so there's no misunderstanding, *I'm* leaving. Oh, don't bother to get up. I'll walk home. Good night. And don't call me again."

She didn't look back.

What the hell was *wrong* with her?

Dillon hurriedly found the confused waiter, got the check and left most of his perfectly good steak sitting on his plate so he could go after Sophie. But when he got out to the parking lot, she was nowhere to be seen, and even after getting into his truck and driving the way she would normally go, he didn't see her.

Where the hell *was* she?

He drove to her house and saw that it was still dark except for the outside light in the front. For the next fifteen minutes he drove around and around. No Sophie. And her house remained dark.

Taking out his cell phone, he called her. The call went to voice mail. So then he texted her.

Where R U? At least let me know U R okay.

Five minutes went by with no answer.

Furious now, he parked across the street from her house. Dammit to hell, anyway. What was *wrong* with her? Why had she gone off on him like that? He hadn't done anything to deserve that. Jeez, women were so emotional! He'd only spoken the truth. Half the time she *did* act as though she wished he'd disappear.

An hour later, she still wasn't home. He couldn't decide what to do. He felt like just going home himself and the hell with her. But part of him was really worried. Sure, Crandall Lake was a small town, but bad stuff happened in small towns all the time. Maybe someone had abducted her. Seen her walking all alone and just grabbed her off the street. Sophie was tough, but she'd be no match for some big guy. Especially some crazy, big guy.

Maybe he should go by the police station. Alert them to the possibility of a problem. He knew Sophie would probably kill him if he did that and it turned out she was fine. But what if she *wasn't* fine?

He was just about to start the truck and head for the station when he saw car headlights approaching and the car turning into Sophie's driveway. The passenger door opened and Sophie got out.

He waited till the person who'd dropped her off had driven off before getting out of his truck and sprinting across the street. She turned, obviously hearing him.

"Where the hell have you been?" he shouted.

"I've been worried sick! I thought something happened to you."

"I'm perfectly fine," she said. "And even if I wasn't, it's none of your business."

"You know, Sophie," he ground out, "I should turn you over my knee and give you the spanking of your life."

Her mouth dropped open. "You…you wouldn't *dare*!" She shoved her key into the lock and pushed the door open.

Knowing she would try to close the door in his face, Dillon pushed in after her. "Who brought you home? Where have you been?"

"Get out! I didn't ask you in, and I don't want you here." She was so angry her voice shook. "And it's none of your business who brought me home!"

Dillon kicked the door shut with his foot. By now, he was breathing hard, too, and he felt like shaking her till her brains rattled. "I don't care what you want. I have something to say and you're going to listen to me!"

"I don't have to listen to you. I said get out!"

Dillon lost it. He'd been so worried about her, so afraid something had happened to her, and he'd been waiting for a long time. And now, for her to act like this, it was just too much. Grabbing her by the shoulders, he yanked her into his arms.

Then he kissed her. Hard. And he kept kissing her. At first she struggled, but it wasn't long before she was kissing him back. Five minutes later, most of their clothing strewn in the hallway, they were making love on the floor of the living room. He shouted as he climaxed, and held her tight as her body shuddered almost simultaneously.

For a long moment afterward, they lay joined together, motionless. Then, sighing, she extricated herself from his arms. Without saying anything, she got up and began to gather her clothing.

"Hey," he said, sitting up. "Come back here."

She turned around. In the half-light from the hallway her expression was inscrutable. "I think you should go now."

"Ah, Sophie, come on. Don't be this way."

She sighed, holding her clothes up against her like a shield. "I'm tired, Dillon, and I don't want another war of words. I just want you to go home. Please?"

One thing Dillon had always known was when the game was over. "Okay, I'll go. But tomorrow? We need to talk."

She didn't answer, but at least she didn't argue with him. He gathered his own clothes, then pulled on his pants and shoved his arms into his shirtsleeves, not bothering to button the shirt. When he walked past her, he leaned over to kiss her goodbye, but she turned her face away and the kiss caught her hair instead.

Still she said nothing until he had opened the front door. And then, just as he stepped outside, she said quietly, "Sex doesn't fix everything, Dillon. Sometimes it only makes things worse."

Sophie lay in bed for a long time without falling asleep. Her body still felt the imprint of Dillon's hands and mouth. And her brain would not shut off. If only she could turn the clock back. If only Dillon had never returned to Crandall Lake. If only she had some kind of sense or willpower where he was concerned.

But she couldn't change anything that had already happened. All she could change were her reactions from then on out.

What was it her mother used to say all the time? *"You can't blame anyone else for your bad choices. All you can do is resolve not to make any more of them."*

Sophie sighed and turned on her side. She'd left her window partially open and a cool breeze fluttered the curtains. *I hereby resolve to cut Dillon Burke out of my life. Permanently. Because he's no good for me and never has been.*

Decision finally made, she closed her eyes and, within minutes, was asleep.

Sophie had always liked Sundays. Normally she went to the eight o'clock Mass at St. Nicholas—her father had been a Catholic, although Joy's father had not—then she spent the rest of the day reading, catching up on laundry, cooking when she felt like it and often, binge-watching a favorite television program.

But today she decided it would be a good

idea to get out of the house. On the off chance Beth might feel like getting away, too, she called her. "Want to see a movie today?"

"That sounds wonderful," Beth said. "Mark is playing golf."

So the two friends went to the local multiplex theater and saw a Judi Dench movie they'd both been wanting to see, then stopped for a burger afterward.

"How's the big romance going?" Beth said when they'd exhausted the subject of Joy and the trip to Hannah's House.

"There is no romance," Sophie said.

Beth frowned. "Oh, c'mon, Sophie. I know you've been seeing Dillon."

"Well, I won't be seeing him anymore."

"What happened?"

"Dillon's getting ready to duplicate his disappearing act, and I have no intention of being the one left behind again. So I told him to get lost. Frankly, Beth, I'm sick of the Burke men."

Beth grimaced. "Well, I can't say I blame you for that, but what makes you think Dillon's going anywhere?"

"He told me Ferguson is on the warpath."

Beth rolled her eyes. "Yeah. The mayor's definitely got it in for Dillon. But he's just so much hot air, you know?"

"You think so?"

"Most of the school board members really like Dillon. I don't think they're gonna go along with Mayor Ferguson. Especially since that new kid who's playing quarterback is so good. I mean, the mayor really doesn't have a leg to stand on."

"That may be, but Dillon pretty much said he's thinking of leaving here anyway. For everybody's good."

"He *said* that?"

"Yep." It still hurt, but not quite as much as it had yesterday.

"Oh, Soph."

"I know."

Beth reached across the table to take Sophie's hand. "I guess he really is a jerk." Beth had never been one of Dillon's detractors. In fact, she'd defended him more times than Sophie could count.

Sophie just sighed. Beth squeezed her hand.

"I'm sorry," she said.

"Thanks," Sophie said, trying to smile. *You'll get over this. It will only hurt for a little while.*

"What're you gonna do?"

"I'm not sure," Sophie said. Then, deciding there was no time like the present, she said, "I'm thinking of leaving here at the end of the school year. Applying for a job in San Antonio…or maybe Houston."

"Oh, no!" Beth wailed. "You can't!"

"I'm sorry, Beth. But you know…maybe it would be the best thing. I mean, especially if I adopt Joy's baby. For his or her sake, it would be really good to have a fresh start. Don't you think?"

Beth looked stricken.

"And it would be better for Joy, too," Sophie continued. She tried to smile but knew the attempt fell short. Thing was, she felt just as sad at the thought of leaving Crandall Lake as she knew Beth did.

"I can't stand the thought of you going away," Beth said. She looked as if she was going to cry. "What'll I do without you? Who will I talk to?"

"We can FaceTime. We can text. We can visit each other. C'mon, Beth. It's not the end of the world."

"It sure feels like it." Beth's eyes glittered

with unshed tears. "We've been best friends since before kindergarten, Sophie."

"I know."

"I will miss you terribly if you go."

"I know. I will, too."

Beth shook her head. "I hate Dillon Burke. If he were here right now, I'd punch him in the nose."

Sophie couldn't help laughing at the image of five-foot-two Beth punching six-foot-three Dillon in the nose.

"Please think about this before you do anything," Beth begged. She began rummaging in her purse for money to pay the bill.

"I will. I have, but I will."

But the more Sophie thought about it, the more it sounded like the perfect solution to her dilemma, for leaving Crandall Lake herself would solve two things: it would ensure privacy for her, Joy and the baby, and it would remove her from even the remembrance of her times with Dillon.

She would begin looking into new job possibilities tomorrow.

Chapter Nine

Dillon drove Aidan to Dallas/Fort Worth Airport Tuesday morning. He'd taken a personal day to do it and decided once he got the boy settled at the airport that he would use the next couple of hours to do some shopping. He needed clothes and he wanted to buy something for Sophie. He knew her birthday was coming up the first week of December, so it was the perfect time to give her a gift.

She'd been avoiding him again. He'd tried to

talk to her at school the day before, but she'd brushed him off. Then when he'd called her, she let the call go to voice mail and hadn't returned it. He'd thought about going by her house last night, then decided to give her a little more time to cool off. No sense rushing things.

Besides, a gift and maybe some flowers would do the job of saying sorry better than anything he could say.

When they reached the airport, they had to say their goodbyes before Aidan went through security. Dillon missed the old days when you could go to the gate and watch people board their plane. Hugging his nephew, he said, "Don't forget—you're going to call me every Wednesday night. And if you have any problems at all, you'll call or text."

"I won't forget."

"And plan on coming back to Crandall

Lake for Christmas." Dillon had considered the possibility of going to Ohio for the holidays, but he wasn't sure he wanted to leave Sophie just then. Of course, she might not stay in Crandall Lake over Christmas. She might want to be with Joy instead. Well, Dillon could always change his plans when he found out what she'd be doing.

Dillon waited until he saw Aidan go through the scanner; then, giving his nephew a final wave, he left. Later, once his shopping was done and he was on his way home again, he allowed his thoughts to return to Sophie. He hoped she liked the gift he'd bought her and wished he didn't have to wait two weeks to give it to her. Remembering the gold heart pendant covered in pavé diamonds and its delicate gold chain, he smiled. Of course she'd like it. It was beautiful and perfect for her.

He could just imagine it nestled against her creamy skin.

Maybe he wouldn't wait for her birthday to give it to her. Maybe he would go over to her house tonight and give it to her as a "sorry" gift. Women liked "sorry" gifts. Certainly, diamonds had always worked for him in the past.

Happy now that he had a surefire plan, he whistled along with the radio all the way home.

Sophie was exhausted. It had been a rough day. Now she had a headache. Plus, she felt nauseated. She must have eaten something that disagreed with her. She decided when she got home, she'd change into her pajamas, take a couple of Advil, fix herself some canned chicken noodle soup and then she'd go to bed early.

She had just sat down with the soup and crackers when her doorbell rang. Sighing heavily, she put down her spoon and went out to the foyer. Peering through the peep-hole, she saw Dillon's face.

No, she thought. *No. I don't want to see him.* Although he would probably guess she was home—she'd turned on the lamp in the foyer because it got dark so early now—she decided to ignore the bell and not answer the door.

Turning around, she walked back to the kitchen. The doorbell rang again, but she didn't stop. He could stand out there all night ringing the doorbell, for all she cared. She was sick of thinking about him and his nephew. *Go away. I don't want to see you.*

Unfortunately Dillon wasn't the type of person to give up easily. Realizing he would be able to see her if he walked up the driveway, she ducked into the hall bathroom. Thank goodness the blinds were shut, but she could hear the crunch of gravel outside the bathroom window. Sure enough, he was walking up the driveway to the back door. He would see the lights in the kitchen and know for sure that she was home. Well, that still didn't mean she had to go to the door. She had a perfect right not to answer if she didn't want to.

A minute later, she heard the sharp knocking.

Go away. Go away.

No such luck. He kept knocking, getting louder every second.

She gritted her teeth. He was so impossible. What did he think? That just because he wanted to see her, that was all it took? That she'd cave? *I don't want to see* you*!*

"I'm not going away, Sophie! I know you're home."

She closed her eyes. He was shouting.

Estelle Pounds, her nosy next-door neighbor, was bound to hear him. Shoot, the entire street would hear him!

"Open the door, Sophie!"

Sighing heavily, and wanting to choke him, Sophie left the bathroom, walked into the kitchen and opened the back door. "Keep your voice down," she said through clenched teeth. "The entire neighborhood can hear you."

"If you'd opened the front door when I rang the bell, it wouldn't have been a problem," he said. Then he grinned, eyeing her outfit. "Flannel pajamas? Really?" Now he chuckled. "Actually, they look kind of cute on you. Sexy."

"Oh, shut up."

"My, we're in a good mood, aren't we?"

"What do you want, Dillon? I'm tired. I was planning to eat my soup—which is cold now, by the way—then head on to bed."

"It's only six-thirty."

"What's your point?"

"Only old ladies go to bed at six-thirty."

"I don't feel well."

He frowned. "What's wrong?"

"Nothing's *wrong*. I just have a headache, that's all. And I'm tired."

"I'm sorry."

He sounded as if he really was sorry. Sophie relented a bit. "So, what is it you want? I really do want to go to bed early tonight."

"I just came over to tell you I put Aidan on a plane today."

Sophie nodded. She'd known he was going.

"And then I stayed in Fort Worth for a while and did some shopping." Now his smile seemed shy. Shy? Dillon Burke, shy? "I bought you something."

Sophie arched her eyebrows. "Why?"

"Why? Because I wanted to. Because I'm

sorry we haven't been getting along well lately and I want that to change." He reached into his pocket and pulled out a small, wrapped box.

For a moment, Sophie couldn't breathe. But then she realized the box was too big to contain a ring, and her heart settled into its normal pace.

"I hope you like it," he said, handing her the box.

Oh God, why did he have to have such gorgeous eyes? And why did she have to feel this way whenever he looked at her?

Slowly, she unwrapped the gift. She'd been right to think it was jewelry, she realized when she saw the velvet jeweler's box. Opening the lid, she caught her breath at the breathtakingly beautiful pendant lying on the white satin interior. "I—I can't accept this," she managed to stammer.

"What? Why not?" He looked stunned.

"Because it's…much too expensive."

"Oh, c'mon, Sophie, it's not. I saw it and I knew it was perfect for you. Of course you can accept it."

She shook her head. "No, Dillon, I really can't."

"I'm not taking it back."

"Well, I'm not keeping it."

"Sophie, quit being so stubborn. There's nothing wrong with me giving you a necklace. Come on, put it on."

"No! I told you. I can't accept this." She pushed the box into his hands.

He stared at her, then slowly and deliberately set the box on the kitchen table. "I'm not taking it back."

"Well, I'll return it to the store, then, because I'm not keeping it."

"That's ridiculous."

"Dillon, listen to me, okay? Just once, listen to me. I don't think we should see each other again. And because I feel that way, I cannot and will not take this expensive gift from you. Now, I want you to leave. I told you I don't feel well, and I really want to go to bed early."

"You're serious."

"Yes."

"I don't get it. Why do you think it would be best if we don't see each other anymore?"

"I really don't have to give you an explanation, but since you asked politely, I will. We want different things out of life, Dillon. That's been clear for a long time. So there's no future for us. And frankly, I don't want to waste my time on you. I want to be free to find someone who wants the same things I do. And if I'm seeing you, I never will."

Once more, he just stared at her. Then, surprising her—she'd expected another argument—he reached for the box with the pendant, closed the lid and nodded. "Okay. If that's how you feel." He gave her a crooked smile. "See you around, Sophie."

Two minutes later, he was gone.

Sophie went to San Antonio and spent Thanksgiving with Joy. She enjoyed the day despite her ongoing malaise, something she attributed to her dejection over both Joy's and Dillon's absence from her life.

She and Dillon had barely spoken in the week since she told him they were finished. She'd seen him at school a few times, and they'd said good morning or hello, but that was it.

During lunch one day, one of the teachers had mentioned seeing him with "a really attractive blonde" at Genaro's the night before, and Sophie had been furious with herself for the way her heart had knocked against her chest and how upset she'd felt.

She had no reason to be upset. She'd given him his walking papers, so of course he would be dating. Dillon would never go very long without some woman hanging all over him.

Who had the blonde been?

Sophie ticked off the names of all the blondes she knew, especially the ones considered good-looking. She knew it hadn't been Nicole Blanchard, because the teacher who had mentioned seeing him knew Nicole and would have said it was her.

Who was it?

But of course there was no way for Sophie to know, so she'd just have to forget about it.

But it nagged at her. He hadn't lost any time, had he? Just proved what Sophie had known all along. She was nothing but available sex to him, because if she'd meant more he'd never have started dating someone else so quickly. In fact, he wouldn't have given up so easily.

With this on her mind, it was hard for her to concentrate on Joy while she was in San Antonio, and Joy noticed her preoccupation.

"Is something wrong, Sophie?"

Sophie started. "Um, no, honey. Why do you ask?"

"You just seem…I don't know. Like something's on your mind."

"Oh, I've just been tired lately. Maybe I need to see the doctor. I might be anemic or need vitamins or something."

Joy frowned, and for the rest of their time together that weekend, Sophie tried to perk up, quit thinking about Dillon and not worry Joy. For the most part, she was successful.

As Sophie drove home that Sunday night, she was grateful for one thing: Joy seemed happy. She'd made friends at Hannah's House and seemed to be looking forward to the future. She had only mentioned Aidan once, asking Sophie if he'd left for Ohio yet. When Sophie told her he had, she'd only said, "Good."

The weeks between Thanksgiving and Christmas break seemed to crawl by. Beth took her to dinner for her birthday, and Sophie did her Christmas shopping, but she couldn't seem to get into the Christmas spirit or over her lethargy. Yet she put off calling her doctor's office. Trouble was, she was pretty sure she knew what her problem was, and there wasn't a pill in existence that was going to make her feel better. Only time would do that.

Two days before the school break would begin, Sophie was in her cubbyhole of an office, working on a report, when there was a knock at her closed door. "C'mon in," she called, thinking it was Lucas Murphy, the editor of the school paper, who'd said he wanted to talk to her about an article he was writing.

But it wasn't Lucas who walked in. It was Dillon.

Sophie's heart thudded, but she managed to keep her voice and expression even. "Hello, Dillon."

"Hey, Sophie."

"How can I help you?"

"Just wanted to wish you a merry Christmas before I leave town."

"You going to Ohio for the holidays?"

"I thought I would. You're going to San Antonio, aren't you?"

"Yes."

"Yeah, that's what Beth said."

Beth? When had he talked to Beth?

"How's Joy doing?" he asked.

"Very well. She seems to really like it there." Sophie considered telling him she was thinking about transferring to San Antonio herself next year, but then decided there was no point. What did she think he'd do? Beg her not to go?

"Well..." he said. "Have a good holiday."

"You, too."

Awkward seconds passed when neither could think of anything else to say. Then, just as she was ready to tell him she needed to get back to her report, he blurted out, "Sophie, I wish you'd change your mind."

"About what?" But she knew.

"About us. I—I miss you."

The ache in her heart—the one she'd been trying to ignore for weeks now—began to throb like a live thing. She wanted to say she missed him so much she'd been making herself sick, but she refused to give him that satisfaction. Because again, what was the point? Would her saying that change anything?

Would it make him say he loved her and wanted to marry her? Of course it wouldn't.

"Can't we try again?" he said softly.

She couldn't, wouldn't, meet his eyes. "I don't think so, Dillon."

Again, there was a long moment of silence. Finally he sighed. "Yeah. I thought that's what you'd say."

Turning back to her computer screen, she said, "Goodbye, Dillon. Have fun in Ohio."

She didn't look at him as he walked out of the room.

Paige Bartlett, Dillon's agent, wanted to meet with him while he was in Columbus. She had come to Crandall Lake right after Thanksgiving, and they'd talked about several possibilities while she was there, but none of them interested Dillon. It was then he'd told her that if she found something good in Ohio, preferably near Columbus, he'd seriously entertain the possibility of leaving Texas.

She'd gotten right on that suggestion. It always amused Dillon that at first glance, people didn't take Paige seriously. She'd laughed that off, telling him it was actually an advantage that a lot of people—men, especially—thought her blond good looks meant she was a lightweight.

"I sneak up on them," she joked.

He'd taken her to dinner at Genaro's, never thinking that it would cause questions. He'd forgotten how curious people in small towns could be. He wondered if Sophie had heard about him and Paige and if she'd thought he'd already begun dating someone else. There was no way to know unless he asked her, and he'd be damned if he would. The most he was prepared to do was try to get her to change her mind about him, and that hadn't worked out well.

It bugged him that he couldn't seem to put Sophie out of his mind. Always before, when a relationship fizzled, he simply moved on.

But that's not quite true, is it? When you left Sophie all those years ago, you thought about her for a long, long time.

Yeah, but he'd been younger then. Way less experienced. And he'd imagined himself in love.

You were in love.

Maybe. Maybe not. He'd certainly gotten over it. Hell, he hadn't been mooning over Sophie.

You seem to be mooning over her now.

Dillon swore. He was sick of thinking about her. He certainly had no intention of chasing her. After all, he had his pride. If she didn't want him, he didn't want her.

She never said she didn't want you. She wants something from you that you aren't prepared to give.

Yeah, well, that wasn't going to change.

And on that final thought, Dillon boarded his plane to Columbus and vowed to put Sophie out of his mind.

Chapter Ten

As she packed for her trip to San Antonio, Sophie decided if she didn't feel better once the Christmas holidays were over, she would definitely see her doctor when she got back.

On Christmas Eve, she and Joy were attending the service at the chapel on the grounds of Hannah's House, and Sophie had brought a black velvet skirt and long-sleeved white lace top to wear. As she pulled the lace top on, she realized it seemed a bit snug across the chest.

Why? she wondered, frowning. She hadn't gained any weight. In fact, the opposite had happened, since she'd been feeling nauseated more often lately. That was odd.

She felt her breasts. Were they *bigger*?

Her hands stilled. Her breasts were definitely more tender. Her heart thudded. *Oh, my God.* Was it possible? She stared at herself in the mirror. Two bright spots of color stained her cheeks, and her eyes looked dazed.

Suddenly dizzy, Sophie sank onto the side of the bed. Grateful the nuns had had a private room she could use for her stay, which enabled her to compose herself before meeting Joy, Sophie tried to get her scattered thoughts together.

All the symptoms she'd had recently: the nausea, the lethargy, the ongoing tiredness—finally made some sort of sense.

Pregnant.

She, too, must be pregnant.

She had to be.

There was no other answer.

Taking out her phone, she looked at her calendar. She studied it, then closed her eyes. A month ago. She should have begun her period a month ago. How had she not noticed?

You were too busy worrying about Joy and crying over Dillon. That's why.

Knowing she had to pull herself together—Joy was already waiting—she finally got up, finished buttoning her blouse and put on some makeup. After combing her hair and finding her black cashmere shawl, she went in search of Joy.

"You look nice." Joy smiled.

"And you look gorgeous," Sophie said. That wasn't an exaggeration. Joy wore a beautiful red wool dress with an empire waist. Her hair was brushed back and held in place with a black velvet ribbon and she wore sparkly black flats. In her arms were several gaily wrapped gifts.

"I need to put them under the tree before we go," Joy said.

Sophie smiled. She'd put her own gifts under the tree in the common room earlier.

All through the beautiful, candlelight service, Sophie's heart frantically pounded in her chest. What she would do if what she believed to be true turned out to be a certainty, she didn't know.

Two babies?

Could she raise two babies by herself?

Or would Joy's baby have to be put up for adoption after all?

Finally the service was over and the sisters walked back to the main house and the gathering that was planned. When they entered the common room, they saw there were already a number of the girls and their guests waiting. A large table covered by a beautiful gold cloth was laden with food, and the tree held dozens of packages beneath it. Soft Christmas music was playing, and everyone was in a festive mood.

Although her mind continued to churn, and she didn't feel hungry, Sophie managed to eat some ham and deviled eggs. She even managed to drink some of the eggnog. She hoped she wouldn't be sorry later. After they'd all finished eating, Sister Monica began to hand out the gifts. Joy ended up with half a dozen in her pile and even Sophie had three. There were lots of exclamations and happy laughter as the girls and their guests opened their presents.

Sophie had bought Joy a new phone with a much better camera—something she'd wanted for a while—as well as a pair of soft leather boots she'd coveted and, as a bonus, she'd also given her a really nice watch.

"Oh, Sophie, thank you!" Joy said. Her eyes were alight with happiness.

Sophie's gifts consisted of a jar of her favorite moisturizer, a pair of delicate gold bangle bracelets, and the newest Maggie O'Farrell novel. "And thank *you*," she said. "I love all my presents."

"When I saw those bracelets, I knew I had to get them," Joy said.

"They're wonderful."

After some carol singing, the party began to break up. Sophie was relieved because she wasn't sure how much longer she would have been able to keep up the pretense of being happy. Not with this possible pregnancy hanging over her head.

Later, as she prepared for bed, she knew she wasn't going to be able to wait until she got home before confirming her suspicions. Somehow she would find a way to get to a pharmacy without having to take Joy along.

The perfect opportunity presented itself in the morning the day after Christmas. Joy said she hadn't slept well the night before and asked Sophie if she'd mind if she took a nap. "I mean, I know you're leaving tomorrow, and I'd hoped we could hit the post-Christmas sales today."

"We'll go later. You have your nap first."

The moment Joy was out of sight, Sophie headed for her car. She found a Walgreens two blocks away from the house. Fifteen minutes later, two pregnancy tests safely stowed in her shoulder bag, she drove back. Closeting herself in her bathroom, she locked the door and administered the tests.

The first one tested positive.

So did the second.

Even though she'd been pretty sure of what the outcome would be, it was still a shock to see her suspicions confirmed. How could this have happened? How could she have allowed herself to become pregnant? It just begged disbelief.

Two babies!

She did some quick calculations. The pregnancy must have happened the first time she and Dillon had had sex. The night she'd confronted him about Joy's pregnancy. Which meant she had gotten pregnant at the end of October. Almost two months ago.

Doing a quick calculation, she figured her baby would be due in late July. Joy's baby would be born in April and would only be three and a half months old when Sophie had her baby.

Dear God.

Sophie put the used pregnancy testing kits

in the Walgreens bag and stowed them in an inside pocket of her suitcase. No way she was going to leave the proof of her folly in the bathroom wastebasket. Then she sat on the side of the bed and thought long and hard.

She had a fairly hefty savings account. In addition to the one he'd left her mother, her father had taken out a large life insurance policy in Sophie's name. She'd used quite a bit of it for her college education, but the rest had accumulated interest and grown over the years. And she'd saved from her salary over the past seven years.

Could she afford to take a year off work? Stay home and raise two babies? Wait to go back to work until the following year?

If she was very careful and stuck to a budget, she could do it.

That night, lying in bed, she made plans. She would go home the next day, and as soon as the holiday break was over, she would give her notice, asking to leave in February so that she could move to San Antonio before she began to show, as well as to be there when Joy gave birth. Since the assistant principal already knew about Joy, there would be no reason to make up any kind of cover story. She would not, of course, let anyone know about her own pregnancy. Well, she'd tell Beth, but no one else.

What about Dillon?

Dillon.

She'd been trying hard to keep thoughts of him at bay. As the father of her baby, he deserved to know. But would she tell him? What if, like Aidan, he wanted no part of her pregnancy? Could she handle that? Worse, what if, out of duty, he asked her to marry him? She couldn't bear that. If Dillon ever asked her to marry him, she wanted the reason to be that he had realized he loved her and didn't want to live his life without her. All things considered, wouldn't it be better all around not to tell him at all?

But what if he found out anyway? And was furious that he hadn't been told? But how would he? If she moved to San Antonio before she began showing, how would he know?

On and on her thoughts raged. And in the morning, she was no closer to an answer than she'd been the night before. The one thing she did know was that she wanted to see an obstetrician in San Antonio before leaving for home. She found one who was part of her PPO and lucked out when she called, because there'd been a cancellation only minutes earlier and the woman who answered the phone slotted Sophie in.

"Yes, you're definitely pregnant," Dr. Kelsey said later. She was the kind of no-nonsense doctor Sophie particularly liked. "I see you're single. Is the father in the picture?"

"No."

"Do you plan to tell him?"

"I haven't decided yet."

"I always think it's best to tell the man, even if you think he won't want to be involved. Saves a bit of heartache later, in many cases."

Sophie nodded noncommittally.

Dr. Kelsey prescribed prenatal vitamins, gave Sophie some literature to read and asked her if she wanted her to recommend a doctor in Crandall Lake.

"No, I'm planning to move to San Antonio in February," Sophie said.

"Okay. I'll need to see you in a month."

"No problem."

Sophie had said her goodbye to Joy before leaving for the doctor's office, so she headed for the highway and home. Already she was feeling better. In fact, it would be lovely to have two babies. They would grow up together and have a close and loving relationship, almost like twins. Plenty of single mothers raised more than one child. She had a good education, great experience and she would be able to hold down a good job. Of course she could do it. Not that everything was going to be easy. She was sensible enough to know there would be rough times ahead, but she'd had rough times before. She was strong. She would be fine.

After she arrived home, the first thing she did after unpacking was call Beth. "Can you meet me for lunch tomorrow?"

"If you don't mind waiting till one. I'm working half days this week."

Beth wanted Mexican food, but Sophie wasn't sure her stomach could handle it and persuaded Beth to have Italian instead.

Beth was already seated at a table in Genaro's when Sophie arrived. Over salads and garlic bread, the two friends caught up.

"I had the most wonderful Christmas, Sophie," Beth said, her eyes glowing.

"What'd Mark get you? A new car or something?" Sophie teased.

"Something even better," Beth said. She grinned.

"Well, come on, don't keep me in suspense."

Beth leaned over the table and said sotto voce, "I'm pregnant, Sophie!" Her face glowed.

"Oh." Sophie was momentarily speechless. "I—I'm so happy for you, Beth." But under the happiness, her heart ached. Beth was pregnant. If Sophie could only stay in Crandall Lake, their children would grow up together and be best friends the way their mothers had been.

Beth frowned. "What's wrong?"

Beth always could read her like a book. Sophie took a shaky breath. Fighting to hold back tears, she said softly, "I—I'm pregnant, too."

Beth's eyes rounded.

"I wasn't going to tell you yet."

Beth put her fork down and simply stared at Sophie. "Holy cow, Sophie. What are you going to do? It's Dillon's, right?"

"Of course it's Dillon's. Who else's would it be?"

"So…you're gonna *have* the baby?"

"I would never consider anything else, Beth. You know that."

"But what about Joy's baby? I thought the plan was you were going to adopt her…or him."

Sophie sighed. The urge to cry was gone. "Yeah, I am. So I'll be raising two babies instead of one." She took a drink of her iced tea. "When are you due?"

"July. July 15, the doctor said. And you?"

"July 30."

Beth laughed in delight. "Oh my God, Sophie. Our kids will be like twins! And they'll grow up together."

Sophie shook her head. "No, Beth, I'm definitely leaving here. In fact, I'm giving my notice when I go back to school next Tuesday. I'm going to move to San Antonio as early as the school will allow me to. Hopefully by the end of January. Before I begin to show."

Beth slumped in her seat. "Oh, Sophie, I was hoping you'd change your mind."

"I know. But this will be the best thing for everyone."

"But…what about Dillon?"

"What about him?"

"He might feel he has a say in this, too.

Maybe he'll want to be a part of the baby's life."

"I don't know if I'm even going to tell him."

"Oh, Sophie." Beth shook her head.

"What? You think I *should*?"

"He's the father," Beth said quietly. "Don't you think he has a right to know?"

"I'm not sure he has a right to any consideration at all." Sophie knew she sounded bitter, but it was hard not to. Dillon had disappointed her so many times.

"You feel that way now because you're still angry with him. But later, I know you'll change your mind."

"I'm not so sure about that."

"But Sophie, don't you think, under the circumstances, he'll want to marry you?"

"I don't want him on those terms."

"What do you mean?"

"I mean, if we were ever to get married—

and don't hold your breath!—I want it to be because he loves me. I want what you have with Mark. I don't want Dillon because he feels guilty or obligated to me. That would be horrible, and not a good way to start out."

Beth sighed heavily. "I understand. I guess I'd feel the same way. But, Sophie, I hate to see you so unhappy."

"But I'm not unhappy! I'm actually excited. My life is going to be so different from what it is now." And if Sophie didn't wholly believe that, she knew it would eventually be true.

"It won't be easy, raising two children on your own," Beth pointed out.

"I know that. But when has my life ever been easy?"

Beth reached across the table and grasped Sophie's hand. "I worry about you, Sophie."

Sophie smiled and squeezed Beth's hand. "I know you do. Thank you. And, Beth?"

"Yes?"

"I'm really happy for you. You know that, don't you? I don't want you to be sad about me. It's going to work out. And we'll see each other often."

Beth made a face. "But only if I come to San Antonio, right? I mean, I can't see you coming here with two babies. Wouldn't the tongues wag then?"

"We'll see. Maybe by then I won't give two hoots what anyone thinks or says."

But down deep, she knew she *would* care. She also knew that no matter how much she had reassured Beth, their conversation had re-awakened her misgivings. She might be telling Beth all would be well and she was happy about her pregnancy, but was that really true?

Weren't her problems just beginning?

And was she entirely sure she could handle everything she would be facing? Especially alone?

* * *

Dillon spent the holidays in Columbus with Aidan. A couple of days before Christmas, his agent called him and invited him to lunch. "I've got a proposition for you."

"Oh? What is it?"

"Let's wait until we see each other, okay?"

"Okay."

Now they were seated across from each other at a popular eatery in downtown Columbus. They had just been served their appetizer and Paige had outlined an offer she'd received on his behalf the previous day.

"So, what do you think?"

Dillon stared at her. Paige had just given him an offer from Penn State to become the assistant to the offensive coach for the varsity football team. His responsibilities would be heavy involvement with the quarterbacks and tight ends. Dillon had never expected an offer like this so soon. He had imagined he would have to have a few seasons of high school coaching under his belt before any college would pay attention.

"Say yes," Paige said. "You aren't going to get a better offer. Not unless you want to go into analysis or play-by-play."

As flattered as Dillon felt by the offer and as much as he knew he would enjoy the job, he couldn't push thoughts of Sophie out of his mind. Did he really want to leave Crandall Lake? Did he really want to say goodbye to her again? "Can I have a few days to think about it?" he finally said.

Paige sighed. "Don't take too long. They're not going to wait around forever."

That night, Dillon took out one of the pieces of stationery from the desk in his hotel room. Always before, whenever he was considering some kind of big change, he made a list of the pros and cons.

An hour later, his list looked like this:

Pros: (1) he would be closer to Aidan and could keep an eye on him, (2) the money was considerably better, (3) he would be doing something more challenging than high school football, and (4) there was a lot more opportunity for advancement than his job in Crandall Lake afforded.

Cons: (1) he would be cutting Sophie out of his life completely, (2) he would be leaving Texas and the hill country, an area he loved, (3) he'd be leaving the first home he'd ever owned, and (4) he would not get to see Aidan's child grow up.

By morning he was still no closer to a decision than he'd been the night before. He and Paige had arranged to meet for breakfast, and he knew she wasn't going to be happy with him.

He was right. "Dillon, I can't believe you're waffling on this. I thought you'd be ecstatic. This offer is everything you'd hoped for."

"I know," he said. He ate some of his pancakes, stalling for time. Finally he decided to be entirely honest with her. "The trouble is, I really don't want to leave Texas. And…I don't think I want to go back to northern winters." He'd almost said something about Sophie but quickly stopped himself.

"Why didn't you tell me this before?"

"I guess I didn't realize how I felt until you told me about the offer."

Paige sighed. "Okay. I guess I'll have to change direction. Or do you want me to stop looking for something else altogether?"

Dillon shook his head. "No, keep looking.

I, uh, might even consider Oklahoma. But I prefer Texas."

Later that day, as he thought back on the conversation, Dillon hoped he'd made the right decision. He told himself Sophie'd had nothing to do with his decision to turn down the Penn State offer, but he knew that wasn't quite true.

All in all, it was a good Christmas for him and Aidan. Aidan seemed a lot more subdued and mature than he'd seemed even a couple of months ago, and Dillon realized Joy's pregnancy had affected him a lot more than he'd let on. Dillon wondered if Aidan was sorry about his decision to leave Crandall Lake and decided to ask Aidan about the situation again. It was three days after Christmas and they were having breakfast together at a local café.

Aidan didn't answer at first. Meeting

Dillon's eyes at last, he said, "I think about Joy…and the baby…a lot."

"Are you sorry about leaving?"

Aidan shrugged. "I don't know. I thought this was the right thing for me, but now I'm not sure. Nothing's the same, you know? I thought…coming back…being with my friends again…everything would be better."

"And it's not?"

"No. Everybody's kind of…moved on. You know?"

Dillon had never felt more sorry for the kid. He had just learned a hard truth: it was impossible to recapture the past. You really *couldn't* go home again. Once your life changed, it was changed forever. "Do you want to come back to Crandall Lake? You can, you know. But if you do want to, you'd have to make up your mind right away. Right now you've only missed a few weeks of school there and you could probably catch right up, but if you wait any longer, it'll be harder."

"I know. I—I've been thinking about it." He played with his napkin. "If I did come back, maybe I could see Joy on the weekends? If she wanted me to. I—I could be there when the baby's born."

"Yes, you could."

Aidan frowned. "But what about the condo? You signed a lease."

"That's not a big deal." Dillon would lose a month's rent by breaking the lease, but that wasn't important—not compared to what Aidan was facing.

For a long moment, Aidan stared off into space. Finally he turned back to Dillon. "Are you sure you want me back?"

"I never wanted you to leave in the first place," Dillon said.

Aidan's smile was slow in coming, but when

it did, it was the most genuine smile he'd ever given Dillon. "I'm sorry I've given you so much trouble."

Dillon couldn't help the surge of pride he felt. Aidan was growing up. "That's in the past. Let's concentrate on the future."

"Yeah." Aidan sighed. "Do you think this is the right thing to do? I mean, it's all settled… and everything. Joy…she might not want me around."

"You'll never know until you ask."

Aidan nodded thoughtfully.

"No matter what she says, you have a right to be in your baby's life if you want to."

Aidan nodded again. "But I wouldn't want to do anything Joy didn't want me to do. I—" He hung his head. "I hurt her enough."

For some reason, Sophie's image popped into Dillon's mind. But he quickly pushed it away. This wasn't about him and Sophie.

She wasn't the one pregnant. This was about Aidan and Joy. They might be young, but they still had a right to make decisions about their lives without interference.

"You know, Aidan, once Joy knows how you feel, she might surprise you. Give her a call. Talk to her."

"I wish…"

"What?"

"I wish I could see her. Not just call her."

Their eyes met again. Dillon searched his nephew's for any sign of doubt. He saw none. The kid really did want to see Joy. And maybe, just maybe, this was the right thing to do. "I could probably get us a flight to San Antonio today."

The spark of hope in Aidan's eyes was all the incentive Dillon needed. He picked up his cell phone and found the website he always used to book travel. Fifteen minutes later, minus a twelve-hundred-dollar hit to his MasterCard, he and Aidan were booked on a two o'clock flight to Houston. They would arrive in San Antonio at eight tonight. Dillon had also gotten them rooms at one of the older downtown hotels. The River Walk hotels were all booked for New Year's.

Surprisingly the holiday didn't seem to impact the airline's performance, and their flight out of Columbus took off on time. They landed a few minutes ahead of schedule at Bush Intercontinental in Houston and had plenty of time to make their connection to San Antonio.

Exiting the plane at the San Antonio International Airport, Dillon wasn't prepared for the heat. He should have been, but the ten days he'd spent in Columbus had made him think it was cold everywhere. He and

Aidan shed their coats and headed for the rental car desk.

It was nine-thirty before they checked into their hotel. Too late to call Joy, they decided.

"I'll just drive you over there in the morning," Dillon said.

"Don't you think we should call first?"

"What if she says she doesn't want to see you?"

Aidan nodded. "Yeah. That's a good point."

"If you just go there, you'll have the element of surprise on your side."

Dillon hoped Aidan slept better than he did. His mind churned with possibilities. He and Aidan had already discussed what they thought was the best plan if Joy agreed. Aidan would finish his senior year in Crandall Lake, spending as many weekends in San Antonio as he could, and he would be there when their baby was born.

After that, everything depended on how Joy felt. And they wouldn't know that until Aidan talked to her. What Sophie would think about this development bothered Dillon, because he was pretty certain she would not be a happy camper. She would be especially angry that she hadn't been consulted first.

But Dillon still felt he was doing the right thing.

And if she didn't agree, if this made her even more furious with him, he guessed he would just have to live with it.

Chapter Eleven

Sophie slept in on Friday morning. She woke feeling groggy, but at least she wasn't nauseated. She'd been afraid the pasta she'd eaten the night before might disagree with her. Deciding she'd feel even better once she showered, she headed for the bathroom.

Forty minutes later, dressed in jeans and a loose cotton shirt, she padded downstairs and headed for the coffeemaker. A few minutes later, steaming cup in hand, she sat down to her laptop.

She'd decided to research townhomes, patio homes and condominiums in San Antonio. Now that she'd made up her mind to move there in March, she wanted to be ready. Mostly she wanted to prepare a budget, make sure she was right about being able to afford to take a year off work and just see what was available.

An hour later, she'd found several complexes that interested her, and was also satisfied that financially, her plan would work. She would have to be careful, of course, stick to her budget, but she was used to doing that anyway. Sophie had never been extravagant. Once in a while, she'd indulge herself and splurge a little—mostly on clothes or shoes—but never to the point that she created a problem. And once she had the babies to take care of, she knew she'd be doubly cautious.

She smiled, touching her tummy. It was hard

to believe so much had happened in just a few short months. In another month, she would begin to show. But as long as she kept her tops loose, she should be okay. Still, it was a good thing she planned to be gone by the first of February. What would Dillon think when he found out she was leaving?

What would he say?

And what would she say back?

Sighing, she pushed the problem of Dillon out of her mind, at least for today. Instead she decided to give Joy a call and see how she was doing. But before she could, her cell rang. It was Beth.

"What're you doing today?" Beth asked.

"Not a thing. Why?"

"I'm gonna go look at maternity clothes. I thought you might want to come."

Sophie smiled. That *would* be fun. And she

did need to get some tops. "Sounds good. How soon do I need to be ready?"

"How about I'll pick you up about ten-thirty? We can have lunch out, too."

"I'd love that."

So the two of them went shopping and Sophie indulged by buying a couple of pairs of pants that would stretch and half a dozen pretty, flowing tops. They stopped for salads afterward, and by the time Beth dropped Sophie at home, it was after two.

She put her purchases away, poured herself a glass of Diet Coke, then sat down at the kitchen table to call Joy. When the call went to voice mail, she left a message, then texted Joy.

After an hour went by with no call back or answering text, Sophie decided to call the main number at Hannah's House.

"I'm sorry, Ms. Marlowe," the operator said, "but Joy isn't here right now."

Sophie frowned. Where could her sister be? "Do you know where she went?"

"No, I'm sorry, I don't."

"Are you sure she didn't tell you where she was going?" Joy didn't have a car, so where could she have gone on her own?

"No, Ms. Marlowe. All I know is, a young man came to see her and she went off with him."

Sophie's heart jolted. A young man? Joy didn't know any young men there. "Who was it? He had to give his name to see her, didn't he?"

"Um, I don't know. I wasn't at the desk when he came."

"Well, who was? Can you check and find out?"

"Hold on a minute. Let me ask around."

A few moments later, the young woman came back. "Um, Miss Marlowe? We had a volunteer working this morning and she's gone this afternoon."

Sophie sighed in frustration. Could it have been Aidan who'd come? Had Joy been in touch with him? No. She would have told Sophie if she had. But who else could it have been? Frowning, Sophie thanked the young woman and disconnected the call. The only way Aidan could possibly know how to find Joy was if Dillon had told him.

Why would he do that?

Anger now fueling her movements—there was obviously something happening Dillon didn't want her to know about—she pressed the familiar numbers of his cell.

He'd better have some answers.

Joy stared at Aidan. The two of them were sitting on a park bench only a block from Hannah's House. Dillon had driven away after telling them he'd be back whenever they wanted. "All Aidan has to do is call me," he'd said.

Joy had been so stunned, first to see Aidan and then to hear what he'd had to say, that she'd barely been able to thank his uncle and tell him goodbye.

"I'm sorry, Joy," Aidan said, taking her hand. "I know I hurt you."

"Yes, you did."

He swallowed. "I—I missed you."

Joy's eyes filled with tears. "I missed you, too," she whispered.

"Can…we start over?"

"How…how is that going to happen? With you in Ohio and me here?"

"I'm only going back to Ohio to pack. I'm moving back to Crandall Lake to finish school. And…if it's okay with you…I'll come to San Antonio on the weekends to be with you. I—I want to be here when you have the baby."

"You...you *mean* that?"

"Yes."

"What if you change your mind again?"

"Look," he said, squeezing her hand. "Dillon and I talked this all out. I told him that being away from you made me realize that I—I really do love you. And...and I want to be a part of your life."

"What about our baby? Do you want to be a part of his life, too?"

"If...you want me to be."

Joy frowned. "How would that work?"

"I don't know yet. We'd have to talk to your sister and Dillon and do a lot of research, but I was thinking maybe I could go to college at UT in Austin. And...and maybe we could get an apartment there and you could finish high school...and if you wanted to...we could keep the baby."

Joy just stared at him. She could barely think. Could he really *mean* all this? It was such a drastic change from before when all he'd wanted to do was escape her and the pregnancy that she couldn't absorb it all in just a few minutes.

"What do you think? I know we'd have a lot to work out, that it wouldn't be easy, but if we both want it enough, we can figure out a way to make it happen."

"Wh-what would we live on? Would you work? Who would watch the baby?"

"I'd probably have to find a part-time job, but I have enough money to last us a couple of years anyway. And Dillon said he'd help."

"I—I don't know what to say," Joy said. Her heart felt so full, and she wanted to believe he was sincere, yet she was still afraid. He might feel this way now, but what if he changed his mind? He'd done that once already. He could do it again, couldn't he? What if she said she loved him, too, and wanted nothing more than to spend her life with him and their baby, and then he got tired of her or things got too hard and he left her again?

Aidan leaned forward. "I do love you, Joy," he murmured. "I missed you so much. If you'll let me, I'll prove it to you." Then he kissed her.

Joy's heart leaped. Pulling his head closer, she kissed him back. When they moved apart, she looked deep into his eyes. What she saw there made her so happy she was sure her heart was going to pound right out of her chest. "I—I love you, too, Aidan."

"So you're okay with all this? You want to keep our baby?"

Now she knew what it meant when people

said they threw caution to the wind, because suddenly all of her doubts evaporated. "I'm more than okay with it. I'm ecstatic!" She still couldn't believe it. Aidan wanted to marry her when she felt she was ready. He wanted to help her raise their baby. She would finish high school with him by her side. They would both work part-time and they would both go to college. They would be together. She hadn't even told him about her Social Security income, the money she got each month since her parents had died and would continue to get until she turned eighteen. He had no idea Sophie had arranged for the money to be deposited into a savings account for Joy and that there was quite a bit accumulated now.

This time when they kissed, Joy knew that it was all going to be okay. It wouldn't be easy; they would have some tough times ahead. But they would face them together.

* * *

Dillon saw on his caller ID that it was Sophie phoning him. He debated, then decided to let the call go to voice mail. He could guess what she wanted to talk about. Somehow she'd found out Aidan and Joy were together. Dillon felt like a lowlife avoiding her like this, but before he talked to Sophie, he knew he had to sit down with Aidan, find out what he and Joy had decided. He knew Sophie would be furious with him, but it couldn't be helped.

"I'm sorry, Sophie," he whispered, looking regretfully at the phone. "But it's all good. You might not think so at first, but everything's going to work out."

Yet even as he said it, he wondered if he was right.

Joy saw that Sophie had called her twice. She hadn't heard the ring; her phone had been buried in her shoulder bag and she'd been so enthralled with Aidan and what he'd been telling her that she hadn't been tuned in to anything else.

Joy bit her lip. "My sister's been calling me."

"Want to call her back?" Aidan said. They were still sitting together on the park bench, but now his arm was around her protectively and every few minutes, he would kiss her again and tell her she was beautiful, and he loved her.

"Later," Joy said. She knew she was being a chicken, but she couldn't help it. She was scared of what Sophie would say when she heard Joy's news. She wanted to think Sophie would be happy for her, but believing that was a different story. "Okay. Are you cold? Want to go back to the house?"

"No, I'm fine. I'd rather stay here." At the house, she'd have to answer questions. Plus, they wouldn't be able to be alone. Boys were not permitted in the girls' rooms and there really wasn't any other place you could go other than the visitors' lounge or the chapel. Neither was a good option as far as Joy was concerned, because neither afforded much privacy.

"I could call Dillon. We could go get something to eat," Aidan said.

"Let's wait a little bit."

"Okay. Um, I was thinking," Aidan said.

"What?"

"If we have a boy, how would you feel about naming him Derek?" Aidan gave her a shy smile. "That was my dad's name."

"Oh, Aidan. I would love to name him Derek. But what if it's a girl?"

"My mom's name was Carol," he said softly.

"And my mom's name was Jennifer," she said. "We could name a girl Jennifer Carol."

They smiled at each other. And then they didn't talk for a while. They were too busy kissing.

Dillon waited another half hour, and when Aidan still hadn't called him, he decided to call Aidan.

"Listen," he said when Aidan answered, "Joy's sister has been calling me and I haven't picked up because I wanted to know what you and Joy and have decided before I talk to her."

"I was going to call you in a little while," Aidan said.

"Okay. So what's the decision?"

Dillon smiled as Aidan explained what they'd talked about. "Okay, then. I'll call her sister."

"Uh, wait. Lemme see what Joy says."

Dillon could hear the two of them talking; then Aidan came back on the line. "She says okay, but she feels bad because her sister's been calling her, too, and she didn't pick up, either. Maybe she should call her first."

"Don't worry about it, okay? I'll take care of things. Do you want me to head back and pick you up?"

"No, Joy and I are gonna walk back to the house. Why don't you come there in a little while? Maybe we could all go have an early dinner somewhere."

"Sounds good. I'll see you in half an hour."

After disconnecting the call, Dillon sat thinking for a few minutes before calling Sophie. Deciding he had to face the music sometime, he finally placed the call.

She answered immediately. "Dillon? Where are you?"

"I'm sitting in my car. Why? Where are you?"

"I'm at home! I've been trying to reach Joy

and no one seems to know where she is, nor is she answering my calls. Do *you* happen to know where she is?"

Dillon took a deep breath. "Yes, I do. She's with Aidan."

"That's what I thought. What are you trying to pull, Dillon? Why is Aidan in San Antonio?"

So Dillon explained, finishing with "I'm sorry I didn't let you know ahead of time, Sophie, but I thought this was something the kids needed to work out on their own."

"Oh, really? You made that decision all by yourself, did you?"

He heard the way her voice shook and knew she was beyond angry. "I did what I thought was right," he said quietly. "If that upsets you, I'm sorry. I think, in my shoes, you would have done the same thing."

"You have no idea what I would have done,

Dillon. One thing I know, though. I would never have gone behind your back."

"Look, can this discussion wait until we can see each other? I'm supposed to be heading back to Hannah's House to pick up the kids and we're going to have dinner together before Aidan and I take off."

"So you think everything's settled? And that I should just be a good little girl—a team player—and fall right into line with your plans? Well, I don't think what you're proposing is a good idea at all. And I can't believe you thought I would! Joy is only sixteen, Dillon! She is far too young to make this kind of commitment and certainly way too young to get married."

"They're not talking about getting married now, Sophie. Not until Joy's eighteen."

"Oh, but it's okay for them to live together until then?"

"Look, nothing's cast in stone yet. We can all sit down like civilized human beings and talk about this, can't we?"

"You never even thought about me, how I'd feel, did you? You just went ahead and did what you wanted to do, the same way you've lived your entire life!"

"I *did* think about you, but I felt this was the kids' decision to make, not yours…and not mine."

"*Kids.* That's the operative word here. They are *kids.* They have no idea what life is going to be like after that baby is born. And you don't, either. You're a selfish, pigheaded, clueless…*idiot*!"

"I'm sorry you feel that way, Sophie," he said stiffly.

"If you think I'm just going to say okay to this stupid scheme of yours, you don't know me at all. Since Joy doesn't seem to want to talk to me, you can tell her that I'm leaving for San Antonio as soon as I get my things together and that I will see her tonight."

And with that, she hung up on him.

Chapter Twelve

Sophie knew she had to calm down. First of all, it was dangerous to drive all the way to San Antonio when she was so upset. Second, it was bad for her baby to be so stressed.

Oh, she could just strangle Dillon! This plan of his and Aidan's was madness. She could excuse Aidan because he was just a kid, and kids had big ideas that weren't sensible or realistic. But Dillon! Dillon knew better. What in the world was he thinking?

If only she could just call Joy and talk to her. But that wouldn't work. She had to see Joy. She had to talk to her in person.

Sophie waited thirty minutes, and by then she felt calm enough to load her overnight bag in the car and take off for San Antonio. She made good time and pulled into the driveway of Hannah's House a little before seven that evening. In the darkness, the Christmas lights made everything look festive. Sophie wished her mood matched and that she was there for a happy reason.

"Miss Marlowe!" the receptionist exclaimed when she saw Sophie enter. "We didn't expect you back so soon. Does Joy know you're coming?"

"She should," Sophie said. She was still fighting hurt feelings because Joy had not called her.

"I'll let her know you're here."

While she waited, Sophie called the little hotel she usually stayed in when she visited and was relieved to find they had a room for her tonight. A few minutes later, Joy entered the visitors' lounge. She looked hesitant, but she came right over and hugged Sophie. Her eyes were bright and filled with hope. Sophie's heart ached, and she couldn't stay mad at Joy. She was so young and naive.

"Oh, Sophie," Joy said, "please don't be angry with me."

"I'm not angry with you. I'm furious with Dillon. This scheme of his is crazy, and it just frustrates me that he brought Aidan here without telling me and that the two of them have talked you into something that makes no sense at all."

"Why doesn't it make any sense?" Joy asked in a small voice.

"Honey, you *know* why. Aidan is only eighteen. He hasn't even finished high school yet. And you're only *sixteen.* You admitted you're too young to be a mother, that you have plans for your life. You're going away to *college.* And so is he. I… You agreed that I could adopt your baby. That that was the best plan for everyone. How has any of that changed?"

Joy bowed her head. For a long moment she didn't answer. When she finally looked at Sophie again, her eyes were shining. But not with tears. With happiness. "What's changed is that Aidan realizes how much he loves me, Sophie. He wants us to be together, to raise our baby together, to be a family." Her voice rang with certainty.

"But, honey, what about school?"

"We're both going to finish school. And we're both going to go to college. Didn't Dillon tell you?"

Sophie sighed heavily. Yes, Dillon had

spelled out their plan. But it seemed like so much pie in the sky to Sophie. She'd seen firsthand what happened when kids thought they could do it all. Life quickly showed them it wasn't as easy as it seemed on paper.

"I know it's going to take us much longer to get our degrees and everything than we planned," Joy said earnestly.

"If you ever *do* get them," Sophie said. She wanted to be happy for Joy, but she couldn't help feeling this was a huge mistake, one Joy would someday regret.

"Sophie, please be happy for me."

Sophie knew when she was beaten. She could see the truth on Joy's face. Now that her sister knew how Aidan felt, what he wanted, there would be no changing her mind. And as hard as it was to accept, Sophie knew these two kids deserved the chance to try to make this work. She only hoped they would succeed, because the idea that Joy might end up being a young, single mother—a young, single, possibly *divorced* mother without a good education—depressed her.

Sophie sighed again. "I guess we'll need to talk to Sister Monica tomorrow."

Joy's smile was radiant. She threw her arms around Sophie. "Oh, I love you, Sophie! Thank you. Thank you. You won't be sorry."

As Sophie hugged Joy back, all she could think was *I hope you're right.*

Later, as Sophie got ready for bed, she thought about everything that had happened that day and everything that had been said. Although she didn't want to admit it, even to herself, she couldn't help feeling guilty as she remembered how she'd told Dillon she never would have gone behind his back the way he'd gone behind hers.

That wasn't true, was it? She *was* going

behind his back. She was pregnant with his child, and she hadn't told him. Didn't *intend* to tell him until it was absolutely necessary. So in some ways, she was just as bad as he was. And he would probably be just as furious with her when he found out what she'd been hiding from him. He and Aidan were still in San Antonio. In fact, Joy had suggested Sophie meet them all for breakfast in the morning. But Sophie knew she couldn't handle seeing Dillon right now, so she'd said she had to leave for home early. If she had agreed to join them, she was afraid he would see right through her. That somehow he would know she was hiding something from him.

So she had a reprieve before she had to face him.

But that reprieve wouldn't last forever.

Sophie was grateful for the drive home—she had some hard thinking to do. This new development had changed everything, not only for Joy, but for her, as well. Before, when Sophie had thought about moving to San Antonio, she'd figured no one would know about *her* baby except Beth…and Joy, of course. That the two of them would be together and they wouldn't have any contact with either Aidan or Dillon. But now none of that was true. Within months, Dillon would be sure to find out about Sophie's pregnancy, because she wouldn't be able to hide it. Also, Aidan and Joy would eventually realize her involvement with Dillon. The kids both thought the only reason Sophie and Dillon had any kind of relationship at all was that they'd needed to discuss Joy's pregnancy.

If only he loved me.

But he didn't. He'd certainly made that clear enough.

Maybe she should just come right out and

tell Dillon about her pregnancy. Tell him matter-of-factly, with no emotion. Tell him she planned to keep the baby and raise it herself. That she expected nothing from him. Nothing at all. In fact, that she *wanted* nothing from him. Nothing he was prepared to give, at any rate, she thought bitterly.

All the way home, she wrestled with the problem, going over and over the same ground. But when she arrived in Crandall Lake, she was no closer to a decision. The only thing she *had* decided was that she didn't have to make up her mind about telling Dillon for a while yet. In fact, it was probably a good idea to give her notice first—that way the die would be cast—and deal with Dillon afterward.

It was depressing to walk into the house after having been in San Antonio with Joy. Sophie hadn't put up a Christmas tree, since there hadn't seemed to be a point. She hadn't bothered to decorate for the holidays at all, and normally she went all out over Christmas. She hadn't even sent Christmas cards this year…or done any baking.

She looked around. This house had been such a source of pride the past few years. It was the first home she'd ever owned. When she signed the mortgage papers, she'd been filled with excitement and hope. She'd chosen each piece of furniture with care, decorated with love and hope for the future. Now that chapter in her life was ending. Soon she would have to sell the house, for it wouldn't make sense to keep it if she wasn't going to live in Crandall Lake.

Suddenly sadness filled her.

Why couldn't things be different?

Why couldn't Dillon love her? Was there something wrong with her? Or was there something wrong with him?

Feeling more and more despondent, Sophie might have succumbed to a crying jag—it was exactly what she felt like doing—but her phone rang and seeing it was Beth, she forced herself to sound cheerful when she answered.

"Hey," Beth said, "are you home?"

"Just got here."

"How'd it go?"

So Sophie told her, ending with "I wish I could be one hundred percent happy for her, but I'm just so afraid this won't end well."

"I know, but what can you do? I mean, I guess you could refuse to give her permission to marry."

Sophie made a face. "I actually thought of that, but it's pretty much a moot point because they're not planning to marry until she turns eighteen."

"Oh. Well, then, that makes a difference,

doesn't it? I mean, if things *don't* work out, at least there won't be a divorce to contend with."

"No, but there *will* be a child."

"Still..."

"I know. I agree. Them living together is preferable to them marrying." She rolled her eyes. "I never thought I'd ever say that."

They talked for a while longer, mostly about the fact that Beth was experiencing pretty bad morning sickness; then she said, "Mark and I have decided to have a small New Year's Eve party and I want you to come."

"Oh, Beth, I don't know. I'm not much for parties."

"You have to come, Sophie. You're my best friend. It wouldn't be the same without you. Besides, this is our first party, so it's special."

"Who'll be there?"

"Just the usual crew, and Allison and Huck—" Allison was Beth's younger sister.

Sophie really didn't want to go, but she didn't want to disappoint her friend. "Okay, what can I bring?"

"Just yourself. Come about eight. It won't be a late evening, I promise."

After they hung up, Sophie decided to quit moping around and feeling sorry for herself. She had just headed into the kitchen to look and see if she needed to make a supermarket run when once more her phone rang. This time caller ID showed it was Dillon. For two seconds, she considered ignoring the call, but knowing him, he might once again show up at the house. Better to deal with him quickly.

"Are you still mad at me?" he said in lieu of a greeting. "Still think I'm a clueless idiot?"

"Yes. And yes."

"Aidan tells me you and Joy are okay, though. That you gave her your blessing."

Sophie should have known Joy would call

Aidan. Probably called him the moment Sophie left. "I wouldn't exactly say I gave her my blessing."

"But you're not going to fight her on this."

Sophie sighed. "No."

"Good."

For a moment, there was an awkward silence. Then Sophie said, "If that's all, Dillon, I've got to go." She wondered what he'd say if she added something like *got a hot date.* Probably nothing. Probably he didn't even care.

"Oh. Okay. I, uh, guess I'll see you around."

"Yeah."

"Okay, then. Well, goodbye."

"Goodbye."

As she disconnected the call, Sophie wondered what he was thinking. Their stilted goodbye had seemed filled with unspoken thoughts. She wondered if he had any regrets where she was concerned. She knew when he was finished with a romantic relationship, he simply walked away. He'd certainly done it often enough. Yet with her, he couldn't do that because they would be eternally connected by Joy and Aidan.

Oh God. I can't bear it. I just can't.

The whole situation had only been bearable because she'd thought she could make a clean break. She'd known it was going to be hard, but eventually she'd felt she'd be fine.

But now…now she knew the truth.

She'd never be fine again.

For the New Year's Eve party, Sophie thought she could get away with wearing her favorite black dress—the same one she'd worn to the homecoming dance—but it was too snug around the top, so she settled for the same velvet skirt and lace top she'd worn Christmas Eve.

Even though Beth had said she didn't have to bring anything, Sophie grabbed one of the bottles of her favorite pinot grigio to take to the party. She might not be drinking, but others would, and she didn't feel right going without a hostess gift.

She went a bit early and was the first to arrive. Beth and Mark had bought a town house, and it looked festive with Christmas lights and decorations.

Mark welcomed her in, giving her a big smile and a kiss on the cheek. "You look great," he said, taking her coat.

"Thank you." She liked Mark. He was like a big teddy bear, always cheerful and smiling. And he adored Beth.

"Beth's in the kitchen," he said, taking the wine. "Go on back."

Beth looked up from her task of arranging little sandwiches on a platter. “Oh, you look nice,” she said, smiling. But there was something about her smile that didn’t quite sit right.

“What’s wrong?” Sophie asked.

Beth grimaced. She beckoned for Sophie to come closer. “I almost called you, but I didn’t know what to do.”

Sophie frowned. “About what?”

Beth sighed heavily. “Mark invited Dillon to come tonight,” she said in a low voice.

“What? How does he even know Dillon?”

“They met playing golf. You know Dillon’s good friends with Alex Lawrence, and Alex and Mark have been playing golf together for years.”

Sophie wanted to cry. “I wish you had called me, Beth. I—I don’t think I can do this.” Maybe she could make a fast exit, before anyone else arrived. No one would even have to know she'd been here.

"But, Soph, what will I tell Mark? I mean, he doesn't know about you and Dillon. You made me promise I wouldn't tell him, and I didn't!" Mark wasn't from Crandall Lake. He'd only moved there three years ago in a company transfer.

"I could tell him I feel sick," Sophie said, but she knew she wasn't a good liar. "See, this is why I could never stay in Crandall Lake. Things like this would happen all the time. I'd be seeing Dillon every time I turned around."

"I'm sorry," Beth said.

"It's not your fault."

Sophie was still trying to decide if she could leave without causing Mark to be suspicious when the doorbell rang with the arrival of more guests, and the opportune moment passed.

Ten minutes later, carrying the platter of sandwiches to put on the dining room table, Sophie saw that Dillon wasn't one of the recent arrivals. Thankful for a reprieve, no matter how short, she greeted the newcomers—one of whom was Beth's sister, Allison—then rejoined Beth in the kitchen.

"What else can I do?" she said.

"Just help me take the rest of the food out," Beth said. She looked extremely pretty tonight, in blue silk pants and a long, tunic top. The color perfectly matched her eyes. She was so happy now—gushing to everyone that she was pregnant. Sophie couldn't prevent the little stab of envy. She would give anything to be publicly happy about her own pregnancy. Pushing away the envy—she *loved* Beth and was thrilled for her!—she picked up a bowl of potato salad and followed Beth out of the kitchen.

By the time the two of them had finished loading the dining room table, more guests arrived, and this time, Dillon was one of them.

She told herself she was cool.

She told herself she didn't care that he was there.

She told herself she was going to get through the evening just fine, no matter what.

But somehow her heart didn't get the message, because it skipped alarmingly the moment she met his gaze. She kept her cool, though, just the way she'd said she would. Because the last thing she wanted was for him to guess how she felt.

Dillon hated New Year's Eve parties. The only reason he'd agreed to come tonight was that he figured Sophie would be there, giving him a chance to see her again. And if he'd been wrong, and she *wasn't*, he would probably have made his excuses and gone home early.

Look at her. She was beautiful and sexy and smart. No wonder he couldn't get her out of his mind. But he was determined to lick this thing, because nothing had changed. She was still a take-her-home-to-mother kind of woman and he was still a no-promises kind of man.

Never the twain shall meet.

He'd better remember that.

At least now—except for the situation with Aidan and Joy—he could feel as if he'd acted in a way he didn't have to be ashamed of. But if he continued to try to see Sophie, knowing their relationship was never going to go in the direction she wanted and deserved, then he would be acting like a first-class jerk.

He watched as she laughed and said something to Beth's sister. How was it possible she could be so beautiful and still look like the girl next door? he wondered. As if she knew he was watching her, she glanced his way, and for a moment, their eyes met.

Something inside him quickened, and he couldn't seem to look away. There was an answering spark in *her* eyes, he was sure of it, but if it was there, it was quickly banished, and all she gave him was a nod to acknowledge his presence. Then she returned her focus to the conversation with Allison.

The competitor in Dillon—the guy who always played to win—wanted nothing more than to walk over there and make her look at him, make her *see* him, make her quit acting as if they were nothing to each other. The other part of Dillon, the part that was a decent guy who really did care about Sophie, knew he couldn't do any of that. If he did, he'd just be feeding his ego without giving a damn about the consequences.

Sighing, he turned and gave his attention to his host, who was offering him something to drink.

"Just a beer," Dillon said, following Mark to the wet bar. A couple of the other men joined them there, and for the next ten minutes or so they talked football, primarily their guesses of the two teams that would be competing in the Super Bowl. Dillon participated in the conversation, but part of him was totally aware of Sophie and what she was doing. She still stood in the doorway of the dining room, but now she and Allison had been joined by both Beth and another woman Dillon didn't know. Above the voices of the others in the two rooms, Dillon could still hear Sophie's earthy laugh, and each time he did, he knew the only way he was going to be able to stick to his resolve concerning Sophie would be to stay away from her. Far away from her. Because when she was close, all he could think about was how much he wanted her.

Once again, just as if she knew he was watching her, she looked his way. But this time there was something unguarded in her expression, something he didn't understand. It was almost as if she was trying to communicate a message, but what that message was, he didn't know. What he *did* know was that it had been a mistake to come here tonight. He should have said no. Because it was now abundantly clear that he couldn't handle being around Sophie.

But how could he leave?

What kind of excuse could he come up with?

"So, what do you think, Dillon?"

Dillon blinked. "Sorry. My mind wandered. What did you say?"

Mark chuckled. "Happens to me all the time. I just asked if you thought the special bond election would pass." The school board was advocating building a new gymnasium and field house at the high school.

"I hope it does. We could use better facilities."

"People hate paying higher taxes, though," one of the other men said.

"But when it's something for the kids, they usually vote for it," another said.

Just then, Dillon's cell phone rang and, seeing it was his agent, he excused himself and walked outside to take the call. "Why aren't you out celebrating?" he asked Paige when she said hello.

"Actually, I'm on my way to a party. Calling you from my cab," she said. "Just wanted to tell you I've had some feelers from the

University of Houston. How would you feel about going there?"

"Depends what the offer is."

"So I should pursue it?"

Dillon thought about how hard it would be to stay in Crandall Lake with Sophie there. How it would always be a constant struggle to keep his distance. How tonight had shown him he was kidding himself if he thought he could stick to his good resolutions. "Yes. Pursue it."

"Okay. I will. I'll call you when I know anything concrete. And Dillon? Have a happy new year."

"You, too."

Dillon disconnected the call and dropped the phone back into his pocket. He turned to walk back inside, then stopped. He really didn't want to return to the party. So why not just go? He could pretend the call had signaled some kind of emergency and he'd had to make a quick exit. And really, did he care what people thought? He could even say he suddenly felt sick to his stomach, that he was afraid he was coming down with the flu. It *was* going around. A couple of the boys on his team were sick with it right now.

Making up his mind, he reversed direction and headed for his car, which was parked across the street.

Chapter Thirteen

Sophie had a hard time falling asleep that night. And when she finally did, her sleep was fitful, filled with snatches of dreams that didn't make sense. Dillon was in a lot of them.

And no wonder, she thought the next morning as she remembered how he'd disappeared from the party. She was shocked when he'd walked out and hadn't returned. She'd seen him answering his phone just before he stepped out the front door, and she'd figured he wanted privacy to talk to whoever had called. Probably that blonde he was dating.

She'd kept a surreptitious watch on the front door, but when he didn't come back, she finally wandered to the kitchen, where she found Beth talking to her sister-in-law, Gail.

"Oh, hey, Sophie," Gail said.

Sophie liked Gail, who was a tall, freckle-faced accountant and the mother of twin boys. But right then she didn't feel like making small talk with anyone. She wanted to tell Beth about Dillon. But Gail was in no hurry to leave, so Sophie had to pretend to listen to the conversation, which centered on Gail's twins and how they were driving her crazy. Finally Gail finished with the subject of the twins and said, "Well, I'd better go check on Paul. He wasn't feeling great and I almost called you to say we weren't coming."

"Oh, no," Beth said. "What's wrong?"

"I don't know. He had an upset stomach," she said while prancing off.

"Beth!" Sophie said in a stage whisper. "Dillon left."

"What? When?"

"Just a few minutes ago. He got a phone call and walked outside to take it. Then he didn't come back."

"A few minutes ago?"

"Well, the call came about fifteen minutes ago. I didn't realize he was gone until a few minutes ago, though."

"Are you *sure*?"

"I didn't go outside to check, but he didn't come back, I'm telling you." Sophie shrugged. "Actually, I think I'm relieved. He makes me uncomfortable when he's around. But still… I wonder if something happened."

"Why don't you text him?"

Sophie shook her head. "Oh, no. *I'm* not texting him. I don't want him to get the idea I care. But you could. After all, you're the hostess. You'd naturally be concerned."

"Tell you what," Beth said, "let's go double-check, make sure he's gone. If he is, I'll see if he said something to Mark. And if he didn't, *then* maybe I'll text him."

So they checked. They even walked outside for a moment, and seeing no one out there—Sophie didn't see his truck, either—they walked back inside and Beth quizzed Mark.

"He has no clue," she said to Sophie when she returned. "So I'll text him."

But there was no immediate answer to the text, so Beth said she'd let Sophie know if she heard from him, and Sophie had to be content with that. Wishing she could leave, too, she instead headed for the food and fixed herself a plate. At least eating was something to do to pass the time. While she ate, she talked to Lisa and Carrie, book club friends of hers and Beth's. Lisa had just finished describing a funny incident from her job as a nurse at the county hospital when Sophie saw Beth beckoning to her from the hallway. Excusing herself, she walked over.

"He just answered my text," Beth said, handing Sophie her phone.

Stomach upset. Sorry. Had to go.

"That must be going around," Beth said. "Gail just told me Paul is feeling worse."

Sophie nodded, but for some reason, she didn't believe Dillon wasn't feeling good. In fact, he had seemed in great form when he arrived. No, he'd left because of that phone call.

This morning, still thinking about last night, she was more sure than ever that something about the phone call had pulled him away. Not that it mattered. And not that she'd ever know.

Because if last night had shown her anything, it had shown her she was absolutely right to believe she needed to stay away from him. As far away from him as she could go without completely disrupting her life.

So tomorrow, as soon as she got to school, she would start the ball rolling and give her notice. Then it would be goodbye, Crandall Lake, and hello, new life.

She just wished the prospect made her happier.

"Sophie, I'm so sorry to hear this."

Sophie nodded. "I know, Connie. I'm sorry to have to do it. But I know you understand." She and Connie Woodson, the assistant principal, were seated in Connie's office.

"I would feel the same way in your shoes. Of course you want to be with Joy." Connie tapped her pencil on her desk. "But why don't you just take a leave of absence? We can get someone to fill in for you, and you can come back after Joy has her baby."

Sophie swallowed. She'd hoped Connie would not suggest this, but she'd known the older woman might. Taking a deep breath, she said, "I can't do that. There's…something else. I—I'm pregnant myself."

Connie's eyes widened, but to her credit, she simply waited without saying anything.

"The father is not going to be in the picture," Sophie continued. "And it will be impossible for me to stay here under those circumstances. I'm sure you'll agree."

"Since I don't know exactly what the circumstances are, I'll have to take your word for it that it would be impossible. But I hate to hear that, Sophie. You're so good at your job. And…I think a lot of you personally, too. Are you *sure* you can't stay? We've had teachers with pregnancies before."

"They've all been married," Sophie said softly.

"Yes."

"Do you really think the school board would approve of me staying on? I mean, I *counsel* girls about not getting pregnant. I'm supposed to set an example."

"The board couldn't fire you for a pregnancy, you do know that? It's against the law, and it would open them up to a lawsuit, which they would want to avoid at all costs."

"I know they couldn't fire me," Sophie said, "but I would be so uncomfortable. This is a small town. And you know how people gossip. No. I couldn't bear it." And if Connie knew who the father was, she would understand even more than she did now. Dillon, of course, probably wouldn't care. Why should he? He was used to being in the limelight, having his personal life out there for everyone to see. But even if he wasn't, there'd always been a double standard. He wouldn't be blamed for anything. Sophie would be the one doing the walk of shame. It was unfair, yes, but it was reality.

Connie sighed, her dark eyes reflecting sympathy. "How soon would you want to go?"

"I'd like to leave by the first of February. I'm already two months along so I'll start showing by then." Sophie grimaced. "You probably think I'm a terrible guardian, a terrible example for Joy and no wonder she got pregnant!"

"I think nothing of the kind. You're human, just like the rest of us." She sighed. "He who casts the first stone…"

Sophie smiled sadly. "You're kind, and I appreciate it."

Connie reached across the desk and patted

Sophie's hand. "Are you happy about the pregnancy?"

Sophie nodded. "I am. I mean, I wish things were different, that the father was involved, but nevertheless, I'm looking forward to being a mom."

"Then I wish you every happiness."

"Thank you."

"Okay, so…February first." Connie hesitated. "If it were possible to go sooner, would you want to?"

"Is that an option?"

"It might be. You know Paula Bell."

Paula Bell was a substitute teacher who had filled in with Sophie's health and life skills classes. "Yes, of course." From what Sophie knew of Paula, she was a great teacher and the kids had all liked her.

"She's expressed interest in a permanent position. She said next year, but if you like, I'll talk to her, see if she wants your job and how soon she'd be available to take over."

Sophie's emotions were mixed. Part of her was excited that she might be able to escape Crandall Lake…and Dillon…much faster than she'd imagined. The other part of her felt nothing but dismay that her life was like an avalanche changing so rapidly, and that she was powerless to stop it.

Connie Woodson sent for Sophie the very next day.

"Paula Bell wants the job," she said when Sophie walked into her office. "And she said she could start as soon as a week Monday."

Sophie left Connie's office with her mind whirling. She'd expected to have a little more time to get her affairs in order before she left Crandall Lake. Still, maybe this was best. A clean, *fast* break. After which she could begin to prepare for her new life.

That night she called a Realtor.

And that Friday, she took a personal day and drove to San Antonio to see Joy. Since the For Sale sign was going up that morning, Sophie knew it was time to tell her sister about her pregnancy, and she didn't want to do it over the phone. Besides, Joy had said Aidan was coming to San Antonio over the weekend, so it was best to get this done today.

When she arrived at Hannah's House, she was told Joy was in her Lamaze class. "You can go in and watch, if you want," an aide said to her.

"Thanks, but I'll wait out here." Even though she would have liked to see what was happening in the class, she didn't want to disrupt things or make Joy anxious.

Half an hour later, Joy entered the visitors'

lounge. "Sophie! When they told me you were here, I thought they'd made a mistake. What's going on? Why aren't you at school today?"

"I took a personal day because I needed to see you. Can we go to your room to talk?"

"Of course."

Five minutes later, settled in Joy's room—Joy on the bed with her feet up—they'd been swelling a little lately—and Sophie in the rocker she'd bought for Joy, Sophie plunged in. "I have something to tell you and, well, I didn't want to do it over the phone."

Joy's expression reflected curiosity but no alarm.

"There's no way to say this except to say it. I'm pregnant, Joy."

Joy's mouth dropped open. "You…you're *pregnant*?"

"Yes."

"But you…you haven't been seeing anyone."

"I know." Sophie closed her eyes briefly. "Technically, I guess I really haven't been. Still, this has happened."

"But who—?"

"Look, I don't want anyone else to know who the father is, because I don't intend to tell him, at least not now. I don't want him to know until it's absolutely unavoidable for him to find out. So before I tell you, you have to promise me you won't tell anyone, not even Aidan. Especially not Aidan."

"But, Sophie…"

"I know. It's a lot to ask, but I have to ask it, and you have to promise. This is really important, Joy."

"I, um, okay. I don't understand, but I promise."

Sophie took a deep breath. "The baby is Dillon's."

"Dillon's?" Shock was written all over Joy's

face. She stared at Sophie. "Aidan's uncle? That Dillon?"

"That's the only Dillon I know," Sophie said drily.

"Sophie!"

"I know."

"But…when? I'm sorry, but this is so hard to believe."

"I know it must be. Thing is, Dillon and I… we go back a long way. We were an item in high school. Remember I told you I understood how you felt when you first confessed to me about Aidan? Well, I *did* understand, because when I was a sophomore and Dillon was a senior, we thought we were in love, too. At least, I fancied myself in love. Not sure what Dillon thought about it. He made me no promises. In fact, he was up-front about the fact he intended to go off to college after graduation, and he did. Pretty much without a backward glance. I was brokenhearted for a while, but I got over it." Sophie had decided it was pointless to go into just how heartbroken she'd been and how long it took her to get over it.

"Anyway, we didn't get together again until after you told me about your pregnancy. I was upset, and I went to Dillon's house to talk to him, and...that's when it started."

"But you never...I mean...did you *date*?"

"We saw each other a few times, went out to dinner when you and Aidan were otherwise occupied. Mostly to talk about the two of you. But, well...things happened." Sophie almost laughed. What an idiotic thing to say, things happened. Obviously things happened if she was pregnant!

"Okay. Things happened. But...I'm confused. Why don't you want Dillon to know? I mean, you two aren't kids."

"I know, but it's complicated. Let's just say that it will be better for everyone concerned if he's not a part of this."

"But, Sophie, how can you say that? He *is* a part of this. He's the father."

Sophie sighed again. Lately, all she seemed to do was sigh. Or cry. "I know, but...Joy, honey, you have to trust me on this. I don't want him to know. Not now. Not until it's impossible to keep it a secret any longer. And if I could keep it from him permanently, I would."

"But, Sophie, don't you think he has a right to know? I mean, you thought I should tell Aidan. In fact, you pretty much told me to tell him immediately. You said he needed to step up, take responsibility."

"I know I did, but this is different."

"How is it different?"

"Because Dillon's a commitment-phobe. He

even said so. And I—I don't want him to feel obligated to ask me to marry him just because I'm pregnant. If he wants to marry me, it'll have to be because he realizes he doesn't want to live without me. I can't accept less. I *won't* accept less."

"Oh. I see." Joy's eyes met hers and there was finally comprehension in them. Comprehension…and sympathy. "You love him. And…you don't think he loves you."

Sophie swallowed and fought the tears Joy's words—and her understanding—had triggered. She wanted to deny what Joy had said, but how could she? She *did* love him. And not only did she *think* Dillon loved her, but she *knew* he didn't. He'd made that clear in every way.

Joy got up from the bed and came over to where Sophie sat. Hunkering down, she hugged her. Hard. "He's a fool if he doesn't love you," she said fiercely. "He could never find anyone better than you."

Now Sophie couldn't stop her tears.

"Oh, Sophie," Joy said. Tears filled her eyes, too. "I totally understand how you feel. You're way too good for him, you know that?"

Sophie bit her lip. She had to get control of herself. Crying never did any good, especially when she was always trying to set a good example for her little sis. She took a shaky breath and fished for a tissue in her purse. Finding one, she blew her nose. "So you won't give my secret away?"

"No. And when Aidan finally guesses… 'cause he will when you begin showing…I'll make sure he won't tell Dillon."

The sisters hugged again, and before releasing Sophie, Joy said, "I love you, Sophie. You're gonna be an awesome mom."

"Ditto," Sophie said.

After that, they talked for a long time, about everything. Sophie told Joy about giving her notice and that she would only have her job one more week. They talked about the house and why they felt it was best to sell it. And finally they talked about how much their lives had changed and would again change once their babies were born.

Later, as Sophie drove back to Crandall Lake, she was relieved to have her talk with Joy behind her. Tonight Joy had shown a maturity and understanding that reassured Sophie and made her proud and hopeful for her sister's future.

Now what Sophie needed to do was focus on her *own* future.

And the sooner she could put Crandall Lake and Dillon behind her, the sooner that future could begin.

* * *

Dillon was glad to get back to school after the holidays. All that enforced gaiety became exhausting after a while. He preferred normal life. The only thing he didn't like about being back was the necessity of avoiding areas where he might run into Sophie. After New Year's Eve he reluctantly concluded that being around her invited trouble. Staying away from temptation was his wisest course. So now his only contact with her was from afar, and that was bad enough.

Why couldn't he stop thinking about her?

He'd never had this problem with another woman. When a relationship was over, it was over. He simply moved on.

But not with Sophie. Every time he saw her, he felt a deep yearning. It was making him crazy, and he was determined to conquer this obsession with her. But no matter how many times he told himself to banish her from his thoughts, he continued to indulge in certain behaviors that weren't helping his cause, one of which was driving by her house whenever he had the chance. He knew this was juvenile behavior, something a lovesick teenager might do, and he told himself he should stop now that he and Sophie were definitely finished, but he couldn't seem to.

That was how he found out she had put her house up for sale. He was on his way to the supermarket, and as usual, he chose a route that would take him down her street. As he approached her house, he did a double take.

A For Sale sign!

He blinked, certain he was seeing things. But, no, it really was a For Sale sign. What the heck was going on? Why was she selling her house? He almost stopped. He could ring her doorbell, come right out and ask her what she doing and why.

But his better judgment kicked in before he could make a fool of himself. For if he did, she would be certain to tell him what she did was none of his business and to go away.

Better to wait and talk to Aidan tomorrow when he came home from visiting Joy. Dillon imagined Joy would have mentioned something about Sophie selling the house, and Dillon could find out what was happening that way. Probably Sophie had just decided she needed a bigger place for when Joy and Aidan and the baby came to stay.

Yes. That must be it.

But if that was it, why did Dillon have this gut feeling that something was wrong?

Joy decided it would be best to tell Aidan about Sophie putting her house on the market. Otherwise, when he found out she was selling it, he would wonder why Joy hadn't mentioned it.

She hated lying to him, but she wouldn't break her promise to Sophie. So when Aidan asked why Sophie had decided to sell the house, she casually said, "She's taking a year off work. She said she can afford to, and after I have the baby, she might finally do some traveling."

She'd thought Aidan might question that explanation, but he just nodded and said, "Sweet," then switched the subject to how hard it had been to catch up on what he'd missed at school. If Joy had offered that explanation about Sophie to a girlfriend, the girl would definitely have asked more questions. Like how odd it was that Sophie would want to travel instead of spending time with Joy and the baby. Or how strange it was that Sophie would sell her house just when it looked as if Joy might be coming back to Crandall Lake.

Men really *were* from Mars, Joy thought with an inner chuckle. They simply didn't think the way women did.

She guessed she should be grateful Aidan had so easily accepted what she'd said. Of course, eventually he would find out the truth—or at least as much of the truth as Sophie was willing to reveal—and then he might be angry with Joy, but Joy doubted it, especially when she explained she'd had no choice.

Sophie's pregnancy was a different story, though.

She couldn't imagine what Aidan would say when he found out about *that*. Especially when he discovered who the father was. Would he feel betrayed by Dillon? She hoped not. He and Dillon had just begun to build a good relationship, and she didn't want to see anything spoil that.

Nothing will. Everything will be fine. Stop worrying.

Joy finally managed to quit thinking about Sophie and Dillon and their problems, at least for the remainder of the time Aidan was in San Antonio. But as she kissed him goodbye, she felt guilty all over again and she vowed this was the last time she would keep a secret from him.

Chapter Fourteen

"She's *what*?" Dillon stared at Aidan, sure he'd been mistaken about what he'd just heard.

"Yeah, I was kind of surprised, too. I mean, I was thinking about it on the way home and I would have thought she'd want to be around after Joy has the baby. But Joy said she's takin' a year off work to travel." Aidan shrugged. "Must be nice."

Dillon was flabbergasted. Taking a year off to *travel*? Sophie, one of the most down-to-earth people he knew, selling her house, quitting a job she supposedly loved, leaving her younger sister and the baby when Joy would need her most? To *travel*? It didn't make sense.

"Was Joy upset by this?" Dillon finally asked.

"Didn't seem to be." Aidan yawned. "I'm beat. I'm gonna go to bed."

There were a hundred other questions Dillon wanted to ask his nephew, but he knew Aidan wouldn't have the answers. Plus, he didn't want Aidan to wonder why Dillon cared. "Okay. Good night."

"'Night."

Later, sitting in front of the TV, which was tuned to a basketball game on ESPN, Dillon still couldn't quite wrap his mind around what Aidan had told him.

None of it made any sense.

What the *hell* was going on? Why was Sophie acting this way?

The only conclusion Dillon could come up with was that Sophie was punishing him. She had decided that if he was so enthusiastic about Aidan and Joy being together and keeping their baby, he could just have all the responsibility for seeing that it worked out well. She was washing her hands of all of it. Including him.

He found it hard to believe that Sophie would do something like this simply to get back at him, but what other explanation was there?

It took him a long time to fall asleep when he finally went to bed. And the last thought he had before he did was that he would seek her out tomorrow, and at the very least, he would make her tell him the truth to his face. He had never once lied to Sophie, and he would make sure she did the same.

Sophie had just finished typing up a set of instructions and notes for Paula Bell, who was coming in that afternoon to meet with Sophie, when there was a knock at her office door. She looked up from her computer, and through the glass, she saw that it was Dillon.

Her heart skipped, and it took all her willpower to keep her voice normal when she called, "Come in."

Why was it that all he had to do was come within two feet of her to cause her hormones to go haywire?

"Hey, Sophie," he said. "Can we talk a few minutes?"

She looked at the wall clock. "I have a meeting at ten-thirty."

"This won't take long."

Of course she knew why he was here. She'd been expecting to hear from him ever since last night, when Joy called her to tell her what she'd told Aidan.

Dillon ignored the chair in front of her and sat on the corner of her desk instead. Sophie wanted to back her own chair up, put more distance between them, but she knew it was better to stand her ground. Putting distance between them would only let him know he intimidated her, and that would give him the advantage.

"Aidan tells me you've quit your job and you're selling the house."

Sophie nodded. *Keep it casual. Don't explain more than you have to.* "News travels fast."

"Why?"

"Why what?"

"C'mon, Sophie. Don't play dumb. Why are

you doing this? I thought you'd want to be as close to Joy and the baby as possible."

"I will be close to Joy and the baby. I'm moving to San Antonio."

"Really? Joy told Aidan you planned to take a year off work to travel."

"After her baby's born, yes, I did think I might do some traveling."

He frowned.

Sophie's heart thumped painfully as their gazes locked. She forced herself not to look away.

"That doesn't make any sense," he said.

"Excuse me?" She managed just the right amount of indignation.

His eyes narrowed. "It doesn't, and you know it. There's something else going on, and I think it has to do with me. What are you trying to prove? That I'm wrong and you're right and you're washing your hands of the kids and their problems?"

Sophie didn't know whether to laugh or cry. She couldn't believe he'd actually come up with this ridiculous theory. "Hard as it may be for you to believe, Dillon, everything is not always about you."

He stood, glaring down at her. "What the hell is it about, then?"

Sophie looked at him for a long moment, and then she stood, too. It wasn't as effective as she'd have liked—he was too tall—but she certainly felt better than she would have if she were still sitting down with him towering over her. "You know, Dillon, I have a perfect right to do whatever I want to do with my own life. And I don't have to explain my reasons to you or to anyone, for that matter. That said, I think we're finished here, so I'll thank you to leave my office and to stop bothering me."

She could see how much he wanted to lash out at her. In fact, he looked as if he wanted to shake her. She squared her shoulders and stood as tall as she possibly could. Ignoring her heart, which was now doing some kind of crazy jig, she told herself not to even blink. All she wanted was for him to go away before she said something stupid.

And then suddenly all the anger disappeared from his face, and his eyes softened with regret. Nodding slowly, he said, “Okay, Sophie, I’ll go. But before I do, I want to say one other thing. If the reason you’re leaving is to get away from me, you don’t have to do that. I’ll go instead. My agent thinks I’ll be getting an offer from the University of Houston, and if I do, I’ll take it.” He smiled crookedly. “I’m sorry about everything, and I wish you only the best.”

Sophie managed not to fall apart until after

he shut the door behind him. Even then, she couldn't let herself cry or scream or do any of the things she wanted to do, because there was no privacy at the school and someone was bound to hear her.

All she could do was sink back into her chair and put her head in her hands and will herself to stop shaking.

The house sold in less than a week. And the buyers wanted to take possession as fast as possible. When Sophie told them she could be out by the end of the month, they were delighted. She figured even if they couldn't close on the deal by then, she could easily drive in from San Antonio to finalize everything whenever she needed to. She should be ecstatic—her plans were working out even better than she'd hoped—but all she felt was a deep regret and sadness for all she would never have.

Yes, she had her baby to look forward to, which meant she'd always have a part of Dillon, but they would never know the happiness of raising their child together.

Ever since Dillon had told her about the job in Houston, and that he would take it if it were offered to him, she wrestled with her conscience. Did she have the right to let him do that without telling him about their baby? Wouldn't he hate her for deceiving him when he *did* find out? And yet…if she told him… and then he felt obligated to her…no, that wouldn't work.

If only he loved her.

If only he'd begged her not to leave Crandall Lake.

If only.

But all the "if onlys" in the world couldn't

change the truth. Dillon did not love her. If he did, he would have spoken up that day in her office. His silence told her everything she needed to know.

Ten days after confronting Sophie in her office, Dillon bumped into Beth at the supermarket. Literally. He came round a corner and nearly collided with her grocery cart.

"Hey, Dillon," she said, giving him a big smile.

"Hey, Beth." He smiled back, noticing how rosy her cheeks were and how her eyes sparkled. Then he remembered. She was pregnant. "You're looking good."

"Thank you." She looked pleased at the compliment. "How're you doing? I haven't seen you since New Year's Eve."

"I'm okay. Chuggin' along." He hesitated, then said, "How's Sophie doing? Sell her house yet?"

"Actually, yes, she has. In fact, she'll be moving in two weeks."

Although Dillon had expected this news—he didn't *think* his offer to leave town would change Sophie's plans—he wasn't prepared for how the actual knowledge would make him feel. He started to say *really, that's great*, but the words stuck in his throat. Something of what he was thinking must have shown in his face, because Beth gave him an odd look. "I...she must be happy about that," he finally managed.

Beth nodded, her gaze speculative. "Are *you* happy about it?"

He frowned. "I...what do you mean?"

"It's a simple question. Are you happy about her leaving?"

"I—don't know. I haven't thought about it."

At that, she cocked her head. Looked at him for a long moment. "Really? You haven't thought about it."

He swallowed. “I—”

“Never mind, Dillon. You don’t have to explain. And I just have one more thing to say. You are, without a doubt, the most clueless, blind and stupid man I’ve ever known.”

And with that, she wheeled her cart around him and walked off without a backward glance.

Dillon thought about what Beth had said for two days. Oh, he was in no doubt about what had prompted her outburst. She thought he was nuts for not snapping Sophie up before some other man claimed her.

She’s right. You are *nuts!*

Sophie was perfect for him. She was everything he admired in a woman, everything any man could possibly want. And she knew all about him. All his faults. All his fears. All the things he’d wanted and all the things he’d accomplished and hadn't accomplished. She made his heart beat faster and she made him happy. He loved being around her. She made him laugh. He missed her when she wasn't around, and he thought about her all the time. How could he even *consider* letting her move right out of his life?

Christ, you really are *clueless. You're in love with her!*

Why hadn't he seen it before? Why had it taken Beth's parting shot to wake him up to the truth?

Damn. Is it too late? Have I screwed up my chances completely by being such an idiot?

The only way he'd know was by asking. And there was no time like the present. But when Dillon looked at his watch, he realized it was already ten o'clock, and Sophie could be in bed. Not a good way to begin. Besides, wouldn't it be smarter to be more prepared to see her? To go with something in hand that would show her how serious he was? Would she say no?

If she did, initially, well, then, he'd beg. He'd get down on his knees and tell her over and over how sorry he was for being such a fool and how much he loved her.

Surely then she'd say yes. Because she loved him. He knew she did. She had to. She wasn't the sort of woman to behave the way she had unless he meant something to her.

He'd go see her tomorrow, after making a few stops at the florist's and at the jewelry store.

And pray in the meantime that it wouldn't be too little, too late.

Sophie left early in the morning for San Antonio. She had to meet with her future landlord to sign the lease on the little garden apartment she was renting and she had an appointment with Dr. Kelsey right after lunch. The lease signing went smoothly and after lunch with Joy, she left for the doctor's office.

Lying on the examining table, Sophie tried not to think about anything negative. She was just superstitious enough to believe good thoughts would help her have a happy baby. She wriggled a bit as the doctor moved the fetal Doppler around her tummy. Today's exam seemed to be taking much longer than the last one had.

"Is something wrong?" Sophie finally asked.

"No. Everything's fine," Dr. Kelsey answered. She moved back a bit and smiled down at Sophie, then helped her sit up. "I just wanted to be sure about what I was hearing before I told you."

"Told me what?"

"I hear two heartbeats."

For a moment, what the doctor had said didn't really register. And when it did, Sophie gasped. "You mean?"

Dr. Kelsey nodded. "Yes. I believe you're carrying twins."

Sophie's mind spun. Twins! Her fraternal grandmother had been a twin, but Sophie had never even entertained the possibility. *Twins!* Wow.

"I know this news might not be what you wanted to hear," Dr. Kelsey said. "Since you're essentially going to be a single mother. Or has that changed?"

"No," Sophie said slowly, "that hasn't changed."

"You probably need some time to get used to this news."

An understatement if she'd ever heard one. She still could hardly believe it. Twins. But really, was that so different from what she'd originally thought she'd be doing? Hadn't she planned to raise both her baby and Joy's baby? The only difference now was that both babies would be hers.

Hers and Dillon's.

Don't think about Dillon. Not now.

"Will I need to be doing anything different throughout my pregnancy?" Sophie asked, pushing all thoughts of Dillon away. "Now that I'm having twins?"

"No. We'll watch you more closely, of course. But everything looks good. Next month, we'll do an ultrasound. And then we'll be able to see them as well as hear them. Would you like to hear them today?"

"Yes." Sophie nodded. "Yes, I would."

So Dr. Kelsey had her lie down again, and this time when she was able to hear both heartbeats, she took the earbuds out of her ears and put them in Sophie's. Sophie's eyes filled with tears as she listened. Those heart-beats were the most miraculous and beautiful sound she'd ever heard. And once again, her thoughts turned to Dillon.

He should be here.

It was wrong of her to deny him this.

Somehow...she had to find the strength to tell him.

When Dillon got to Sophie's house, no one answered the door. He hadn't called first because he hadn't wanted her to tell him not to come. Could she be home and simply pretending she wasn't because she didn't want to see him? She'd done that once before.

He decided to walk around the house and peer through the windows. There wasn't a sign of life. And looking through the back door, he could see that the kitchen was spotless and quiet.

She wasn't home.

Damn. What should he do?

I'll wait. I'll get in the truck and I'll sit there and I'll wait.

What if she doesn't come home?

She has to come home. She still lives here.

She probably just went out shopping or something. She'd be home soon. Dillon checked his watch. It was one-thirty. It had taken him longer than he'd thought to get the things he planned, especially since he'd had to drive into San Marcos to find the Neil Lane ring he wanted.

By three o'clock, he was wondering if he should leave and try again later. But no, if he left he might miss her.

Better to just wait.

At four o'clock his patience was rewarded, and her car came up the street. He wasn't sure if she'd seen him or not, because she pulled into her driveway and into the garage without looking behind her. It wasn't until she'd stepped out that she acknowledged him walking up the driveway toward her.

He saw the surprise on her face, followed by something else, some emotion he couldn't identify. Dillon's heart beat faster as he took her in. She looked beautiful in her dark green coat and high-heeled leather boots, her bright hair a curly halo around her face.

"Hello, Dillon," she said quietly.

He smiled at her. "Hello, Sophie."

"I didn't think I'd see you again before I moved." She eyed the bouquet of red roses he carried but didn't comment on them.

"I know, but I…there's something I need to tell you. To ask you," he corrected himself.

"Oh?"

"Um, Sophie, could we go inside? I, uh…" He didn't want to hand her the flowers and get down on his knees out here where her neighbors and anyone else driving by could see him. If she rejected him, and he made a fool of himself, he'd rather do it inside, in private.

She considered his request for a minute, then said, "Sure. Let's go in."

Following her through her back door, he caught a whiff of the light scent she wore, and his gut twisted. What if she said no? What if she told him he'd blown any chance he ever had with her and to get lost? She wouldn't do that. Would she?

If she does, you deserve it.

When they were inside, she removed her coat and slung it over the back of one of her kitchen chairs. She wore a russet outfit, a skirt and sweater that hugged her sexy curves. Just looking at her made him want to pull her into his arms and kiss her senseless.

"Sophie, I—"

Cutting him off, she said, “Would you like something to drink? I’m parched. I just drove back from San Antonio.”

“Oh? You went to see Joy?”

“That and other things.” She smiled, but the smile didn’t reach her eyes. “I signed a lease on a garden apartment today. It’s only about fifteen minutes away from Hannah’s House, so I’ll be close to Joy.” Walking over to the refrigerator, she took out a pitcher of iced tea. “I’m going to have some. Do you want a glass?”

“No. I just want to say what I have to say. I—I brought you these flowers.” Dillon had never felt so unsure of himself. All the years of dating supermodels and actresses didn’t come close to preparing him for this moment. Every bit of confidence he had seemed to have flown out the window. This woman had reduced him to a stammering mess.

She didn't reach for the flowers, just calmly poured herself a glass of tea. When she finally looked at him, she said, "They're lovely, but what are they? Some kind of peace offering?"

Dillon swallowed. It was time to quit messing around and go for broke. Because she wouldn't take the flowers and he wanted his hands free, he put them on the table. Then he walked over to her, took the glass out of her hand, put *it* on the table, too, and took her hands in his. "They're not a peace offering. Red roses stand for love. That's what the florist told me. I'm trying to tell you that I love you, Sophie. I realized that yesterday, and it's something I should have realized a long time ago. Maybe I did, but I was afraid to admit it. I love you and I don't want to live without you."

Letting go of her hands, he reached into his pocket and drew out the velvet box containing the two-carat diamond ring he'd purchased earlier. Then he dropped to one knee and held out the box. "You would make me the happiest and proudest man in the world if you'd agree to be my wife."

She stared at him. Her gold-flecked eyes never moved from his. After what seemed like an eternity, she finally said, "Are you sure, Dillon?"

"I've never been more sure of anything in my life." And at that moment, he knew it was true. "God, Sophie, I've been such a fool." Getting up again, he pressed the velvet ring box into her hand. "I love you with all my heart."

"Oh, Dillon," she said, and now tears sprang into her eyes. "I love you, too. I always have. And I—I would be honored to be your wife."

Because he couldn't wait, he drew her into his arms and kissed her. They kissed again and again, and when they finally stopped, she opened the ring box. “Oh,” she said when she saw the ring. “It’s gorgeous.”

“Let’s put it on,” he said. “I guessed at the size.”

The ring was just a little too big, but he assured her they could go back to the jeweler’s the next day and have it sized. After admiring the way it looked on her hand for a while, she found a vase and filled it with water. “I love my roses,” she said, arranging them in the vase. “I was only pretending not to like them before.”

He grinned. “Punishing me for being such a fool.”

She laughed. “Yes.” Then she tilted her head and studied him. “What *did* make you finally realize you loved me?”

“It wasn’t a what, it was a person.”

“Oh?”

"Yeah, Beth. Ran into her at the store the other day and she told me I was a blind, stupid, clueless idiot."

"Really? What else did she tell you?"

"Nothing else. Trust me, that was enough."

Sophie grinned. "A blind, stupid, clueless idiot. I like that."

"Yeah, I'm sure you do." Because he could hardly stand being separate from her, he put his arms around her again. After more kissing, he murmured, "Let's go make up for some lost time."

She laughed softly. "Maybe in a little bit. Right now I have something to tell you."

"You haven't changed your mind already?"

"Don't worry. It's nothing like that. It's very good news. At least, I hope you'll think so."

And then she told him.

Epilogue

One year later...

Sophie looked around her kitchen with satisfaction. She loved the house she and Dillon had bought near the medical center in Houston. It was convenient to the university where he now worked and had wonderful green areas and schools. Sophie wasn't sure when she would go back to work; right now she was happy being home with the twins, but she knew one day she'd want to counsel again.

She looked over at the babies, who were both sound asleep in the double pram that had been a gift from Beth and Mark. While she watched, David Marshall Burke stirred and smiled in his sleep. She grinned. At six months, he was a handful and the spitting image of his father, down to the almost-black hair and vibrant blue eyes. His sister, Riley Ann Burke, who took after Sophie with her red hair and smaller frame, was much more easygoing. If Sophie had any regrets, it was that her mother was not around to spoil the twins. Riley had been her mother's maiden name, and since Joy had chosen her mother's first name for their daughter Jennifer, Sophie was happy to settle on Riley.

Sophie smiled again, thinking of Aidan and Joy. So far, all was well with them. They were living in Houston, too, because Joy had wanted to be close to Sophie and Dillon, and

Aidan had no problem getting accepted at the University of Houston. Joy had put Jennifer in day care and was going to school full-time now.

Sophie's life wasn't perfect. When had it ever been? There were days when Sophie felt overwhelmed and tired, but she knew that was normal. After all, she had two babies! And some nights she didn't get a good night's sleep. But she was happier than she'd ever been and thanked God every day for her blessings.

Just then, her tallest and most demanding blessing walked in the back door. "Hey," he said, dropping a kiss on her upturned mouth.

"Hey," she said. "You're home early."

"Yeah, we let the guys go after drills." He put his arms around her, his hands sliding down to cup her bottom. Affecting an Irish accent, he nuzzled her ear. "Thought maybe

I'd have the luck of the Irish today and would find you taking a nap."

Her heart quickened as the heat of his hands reminded her how much she loved him, and how much she loved making love with him. She hoped that never changed. "If we hurry, you could still get lucky," she murmured, pulling him closer.

"Then quit talking, woman, and let's go before they wake up."

So they did.

And although they couldn't know it then, nine months later Sophie would give birth to their second son, and they would name him Braden after Dillon's father.

And they would all live happily-ever-after.

* * * * *